STAGE FRIGHT

ALSO BY
WENDY PARRIS

Field of Screams

STAGE FRIGHT

WENDY PARRIS

DELACORTE PRESS

Text copyright © 2024 by Wendy Parris
Jacket art copyright © 2024 by Matt Schu

All rights reserved. Published in the United States by Delacorte Press,
an imprint of Random House Children's Books,
a division of Penguin Random House LLC, New York.

Delacorte Press is a registered trademark and the colophon
is a trademark of Penguin Random House LLC.

rhcbooks.com

Educators and librarians, for a variety of teaching tools,
visit us at RHTeachersLibrarians.com

Library of Congress Cataloging-in-Publication Data is available upon request.
ISBN 978-0-593-80799-6 (trade pbk.) — ISBN 978-0-593-80800-9 (ebook)

The text of this book is set in 12.5-point Adobe Caslon Pro.
Interior design by Jade Rector

Printed in the United States of America
1st Printing
First Edition

TO WILL AND DELANEY

CHAPTER ONE

AS THE SMALL PLANE DESCENDED, BREAKING THROUGH the dark thunderclouds, Avery O'Reilly finally got a good look out the window.

Below her spread a patchwork quilt of Midwestern farm fields, the green squares defined by gray roads and dotted with the occasional white house and red barn. Her eyes followed the watery squiggle that was Clear Creek as the landscape gently gave way to the familiar landmarks of her hometown. She pressed her palm to the glass. There was the shockingly turquoise rectangle of the local pool where she and Paige used to have swim meets. Nearby, its trees looking like broccoli tops, was

Center Park, where she and Jaylen had gotten stuck atop the carnival Ferris wheel. And beyond that, the L-shaped black tar roof of Lincoln Elementary, where she and Tyler had partnered on every school project from kindergarten through fourth grade.

"I'm back!" Avery whispered.

The plane banked and tilted. From beneath her came the rumbling vibration of the landing gear going down.

Ms. Choi, the middle-aged businesswoman seated next to her, smiled. "Someone will be here to meet you, right, hon?"

"Oh yes." Avery pushed her tortoiseshell glasses up the bridge of her nose. "My best friend, Paige, and her sister."

"Well, I hope you have a wonderful vacation. There is something special about spending time with the people you grew up with." Ms. Choi closed her laptop and stowed it in her briefcase. "You know the saying— 'Make new friends, but keep the old. One is silver and the other gold.'"

Avery considered this. She agreed . . . sort of. Her old friends were definitely gold. But since she'd moved to Philadelphia, she hadn't made any friends she would rate as silver . . . or even bronze. Maybe plastic? Nobody new would ever measure up to Paige, Jaylen, and Tyler. The four of them had been inseparable since before she could remember. If only her parents hadn't ripped her away from them, uprooting the whole family for their stupid jobs. Like they hadn't had perfectly fine professorships in Illinois.

Avery took a relaxing breath. She should live in the moment, like Tyler said to do. He was chill like that. These next two weeks of summer were going to be the best *ever*, and she shouldn't wreck them by dwelling on how miserable she'd been the past year in Philadelphia.

The plane bumped slightly as it hit the runway. Static buzzed over the address system, followed by the cheerful voice of the flight attendant. Avery only half listened. She switched her cell phone off airplane mode, anticipating texts from Paige to explode across the screen.

There was only one text.

From her mom.

> Hope the thunderstorms didn't delay you!
> Don't forget to text me when you land!

Avery frowned. Her seven excited messages to Paige from the morning had been delivered. Paige should've texted back as soon as her half-day gymnastics camp was over. Worry whispered in her ear. Lately Paige hadn't been as responsive as usual. What if she wasn't as thrilled as Avery about this visit?

Reason whispered back. Paige had spent a month up at her grandparents' cabin in Northern Wisconsin, where Wi-Fi and cell service were spotty. And the last few weeks she'd been way busy with gymnastics camp. Everything was fine.

Her anxiety quashed for the moment, Avery texted her mom.

Here

Immediately three dots pulsed across the bottom of her screen. Avery rolled her eyes. Clearly, Mom had been monitoring her phone, anxiously hoping to hear from her. While waiting for the text to come through, Avery pulled her bright red-and-yellow backpack from under the seat in front of her and stood. She was still small enough that she didn't have to bend to avoid cracking her head on the overhead compartment. That was probably the only good thing about being short.

Her phone buzzed.

> Have a great time, sweetheart, and stay safe! Please tell everyone on the block that Dad and I say hi. And remember to give Mrs. Sernett the hostess gift I sent as soon as she's home from the wedding!

Avery's mouth twisted. There was no way she'd forget the shoebox-sized present her mom had shoved into her suitcase at the last minute. That reminded her. She unzipped her backpack and, pushing aside the latest Lark and Ivy mystery book, searched inside for a small gold gift bag until she found it. Whew. The friendship bracelet hadn't fallen out or disappeared. She'd spent hours carefully braiding it using Paige's favorite color combo: neon yellow, orange, and green. Avery rubbed the matching bracelet around her wrist. Paige would love them.

Her phone buzzed again. Another message from her mom.

> Maya from down the block dropped off a birthday party invite for you! Something to look forward to when you get home!

Avery swiped out of the thread. Maya wasn't exactly part of the mean girls' clique at her new school, but it wasn't like she'd ever jumped to Avery's defense when the others mocked her Midwestern accent. Maya's parents were probably making her include Avery on the invite list just because they were neighbors.

She tucked her phone into her backpack and pictured Paige waiting in the terminal with a massive Welcome Home sign. She couldn't wait to give her a huge hug.

Ten minutes later Avery stood alone in the tiny municipal airport, a pit in her stomach. Aside from a grumpy old guy in a ballcap lecturing a ticket agent, no one was there.

She pulled out her phone and tapped out a text.

> where r u

Avery waited a minute, but no answer came. She wandered to baggage claim, losing herself in a cloud of what-ifs. Paige's eighteen-year-old sister Natalie was supposed to be driving her to the airport. What if Nat had forgotten? Or the car had broken down? Or, worse, there'd been an accident? She dug her fingernails into her palm, trying to stop her mind from spinning out of control.

Her phone vibrated in her other hand. It was a text from Paige. Finally.

> Sorrysorrysorry

> . . .

Avery held her breath.

> long story j and laila r picking u up

Avery exhaled.

> see u at my house

Of course everything was fine.

After gathering her overstuffed suitcase from one of the two baggage carousels and waving goodbye to Ms. Choi, Avery stepped through the airport's automatic exit doors. The August rain had stopped, leaving the air damp and surprisingly cool. Her eyes swept over the half-dozen cars waiting in the passenger pick-up lane. None looked familiar.

A rusty little sedan rattled up to the end of the line,

horn blaring. The passenger door swung open. Jaylen, an energetic thirteen-year-old with dark brown skin, bounded onto the pavement.

"Aves!" he shouted, waving madly.

Avery's heart swelled with affection. Jaylen did everything big. She jogged toward him, taking in his Chicago Bears T-shirt, his short braids, his gap-toothed smile. Good old Jaylen. He met her halfway, grabbed her bag, and patted her on the head.

"Still short, I see," he said.

"Still rude, I see," she fired back, elbowing him in the ribs.

He grinned and tossed her bag in the trunk. "Sit up front."

Avery opened the passenger door. "Hey, Laila," she said to Jaylen's big sister.

"Hey, girl." Laila lifted her purple sunglasses up to her forehead and gazed at Avery with her huge dark eyes. "I don't know why you want to spend a vacation in this hick town, but welcome anyway."

Avery giggled and climbed in.

"Boo!" The deep, unfamiliar voice came from behind her. A ghostly pale face shot up over the back seat. "Surprise!" said Tyler.

Avery slapped her palm to her chest. "You scared me!"

"Ha!" Jaylen plopped into the seat next to him.

Tyler jabbed his thumb at Jaylen. "It was his idea, not mine."

"Of course it was," Avery said fondly as Laila pulled the car away from the curb. Jaylen was always up to mischief, and Tyler always good-naturedly went along. But something about Tyler was different. The last time Avery had actually spoken with him instead of texted was during spring break. Back then he'd sounded the same as always—sort of nasal and high-pitched. Now Tyler's voice made her think of a TV newscaster crossed with a bullfrog. "Um, what's up with your voice?"

"Right?" Jaylen smirked. "Bruh, it's sooo weird."

"Well, sorry your voice hasn't changed yet." Tyler flipped his mop of dirty-blond hair.

A flicker of irritation ran across Jaylen's face. He pushed Tyler. Tyler pushed back.

"All right, calm down," said Laila, steering the car onto the highway.

"Not that I don't want to see you guys," Avery said, "but where's Paige?"

"She's . . . wait for it." Tyler paused. "At the mall."

"No, really," Avery said. What a joke. She and Paige

had always agreed there were so many more interesting things to do than hang out at a mall.

"Really," Jaylen said. "Something about buying fall clothes? I don't know."

Avery clicked her tongue in disbelief. They must have it wrong. Shopping would never be part of the "long story" Paige said had prevented her from coming to the airport.

"So, guys," Laila said, "what are your plans tonight?"

"Plans?" Avery shrugged. The boys' expressions remained blank. Paige was the group's planner.

"Wait, I know!" Jaylen pounded on the seat. "We should go see that new movie *The Séance*."

"The one that freaked out Russell?" Tyler asked.

"Yeah! You know if he was scared, it's gotta be sick." Jaylen's brother, Russell, was a local hero. Not only was he the star quarterback at the nearby university, but he'd once actually saved an old lady from a burning building. Jaylen worshipped him. "Bet it won't get to me, though."

"Sure, *you're* braver than Russell," Laila said sarcastically.

"I am!" Jaylen said. "I'm braver than he was at my age, at least."

Avery wrinkled her nose. "*The Séance?*"

"It's only a movie," Tyler said reassuringly.

Jaylen tousled Avery's stick-straight brown bob, messing up her center part. "Aw, she's still a scaredy-cat."

"I am not," said Avery, rearranging her hair into even curtains on either side of her face. "I'd just rather watch a comedy. I'm sure Paige would, too."

"No, she'll be up for it," Jaylen said, tapping his fingertips on his knee. As a drummer, he constantly tried out new beats. "She's way into slasher movies now."

Avery snorted. "I don't believe it." She knew her best friend.

"Wait and see," Jaylen said.

Their short stint on the four-lane highway ended, and they drove along a lonely road at the edge of town. The few buildings were scattered and dilapidated. Ahead, a clump of trash littered the weedy parkway. As the car got closer, Avery realized that the trash was actually some kind of arrangement, with a teddy bear, a bouquet of carnations, and a white poster board dingy with road dust.

WE REMEMBER was written in thick black marker on the board.

"What's that?" Avery asked, pointing out the windshield.

"Speaking of horror . . . ," Jaylen said.

"It's a memorial," Laila explained. "It's been ten years since that kid Maddie died."

"Who?" As the car passed the sign, Avery peered beyond it at the hulking redbrick building set back from the road. A chain-link fence surrounded it. Boards covered its doors and windows.

The desolate scene nudged Avery's memory. "Oh." The air swooshed from her mouth. "Right."

Everyone fell silent.

Even though it had happened when she was a toddler, Avery knew the story about the Old Winter Playhouse. It had been really popular when it was built in the late 1800s, featuring traveling vaudeville shows and musicals. But it had been closed for decades before a local theater troupe had decided to revive it ten years before, when she was a little kid. One summer night that year, when the actors had finished rehearsal for the final play of their first season, a tragic accident had occurred. The director's nine-year-old daughter, Maddie, had climbed onto the catwalk high above the stage and fell to her death. The show was canceled. The theater shuttered. The building had stood vacant ever since, decaying bit by bit over the years.

There were whispers that the place was haunted.

Avery barely contained a shiver. "Who made the memorial? Didn't Maddie's family move away?"

"My mom says nobody knows," Tyler said, his deep voice now subdued. His mom had been there the night of the tragedy, volunteering in the box office. "It just appeared last week."

Jaylen sighed. "There haven't been any Maddie sightings in forever."

"You know why?" Tyler said. "They put in a ghost light to keep her away."

"Really?" Laila perked up.

"What is a ghost light?" Avery asked.

"It's an old theater tradition." Laila waved her hand airily. She was in all the plays at the high school and planned to study acting in college. "Supposedly it's to repel ghosts. But really, it's a safety light they leave lit onstage after everyone goes home at night. So nobody comes into a totally dark theater the next day and trips over props or equipment or falls off the stage."

"Yeah, well, my mom says the owners are super-stitious people," Tyler said. "Plus, they'd do anything to stop the ghost rumors."

Jaylen leaned forward and clutched the headrest behind Avery. "I heard that before they boarded up the building, people used to see Maddie's ghost pressed against the glass doors, banging her fists and wailing like she wanted to get out," he said in a hushed voice.

"Jaylen, don't spook Avery," Tyler teased.

Avery scoffed. "I'm not spooked!"

Jaylen went on. "Russell told me sometimes you can hear a little girl begging people to come in and play."

"You can?" Now that creeped Avery out.

"Stop it," Laila interjected. "You three were too little to remember when that Maddie girl died, but I was going into second grade. It was a huge deal. And *very* sad."

Though the theater was in the rearview mirror now, Avery sensed its gloomy presence lurking behind them, could imagine a lonely little girl's voice pleading for play-mates. When she was six years old, a babysitter named Lizzy had told her that Maddie's ghost attacked kids who left their beds at night. Avery had nightmares for weeks after that. It wasn't until years later she realized that Lizzy had wanted to frighten her enough to keep her from leaving her room after bedtime.

Avery pushed the memory aside, along with all thoughts of ghosts and abandoned theaters.

It was time to focus on making this the best summer vacation ever.

CHAPTER TWO

AS LAILA STEERED THE CAR ONTO RIDGE ROAD, AVERY bounced in her seat eagerly. She was home! And the old neighborhood was exactly the same.

Except . . . the Jacksons' Victorian house, once a cheerful robin's-egg blue, had been painted a dull gray-green color. The massive maple tree on the corner, the one the kids always used as their base for hide-and-seek, had been chopped down. An unfamiliar, floppy-eared dog barked at the car from the McGregors' walkway—could it be that their ancient sheepdog, Cousin It, had finally passed on and been replaced? As Avery opened her mouth to ask, her former house came into view, and the question died in her throat.

A stranger's minivan was parked along the curb in front, and an unfamiliar purple tricycle lay on its side under the crooked pine tree. Her mom's favorite lilac bush by the front door had been ripped out, resulting in an ugly bare spot on the lawn. Instead of ruffly yellow curtains, a boring gray shade hung in what used to be her little sister Julia's bedroom window.

Sadness pierced Avery's heart. The two-story brick house looked smaller than she remembered.

Laila pulled the car into her family's driveway across the street. "Jaylen, carry Avery's stuff over to the Sernetts'," she ordered, popping the trunk open with a push of a button. She scrambled out of the car. "I've got to get ready for work."

"Thanks for picking me up," Avery said.

"No problem," Laila called. "Have fun, guys. And be safe." She disappeared into the rambling one-story house.

As the rest of them exited the car, Jaylen clutched his belly. "I'm weak with hunger. I don't actually have to help you, do I, Aves?" He staggered around the driveway.

"Really?" Tyler squinted down his nose. Although he wasn't as athletic as Jaylen, he towered over him. "That's why you're weak?"

Jaylen pulled himself up to his full height and squared his jaw. "Listen—"

"I'm just playing." Tyler raised his hands in surrender.

"Whatever," Jaylen mumbled.

"Guys, guys, I'll tell you what." Avery pulled her suitcase from the trunk, aiming to break the tension. "Get a snack, I'll get Paige, and we can meet in the tree house in a few."

"Oh." Tyler lowered his arms. "My tree house?"

"Where else?" Avery paused, her hand on the lid of the trunk.

Jaylen scratched the back of his head and shot Tyler a glance. "I guess we could do that?"

"You *guess*?" Avery slammed the trunk closed. "We always meet there."

"Fine, let's do it." Tyler clapped Jaylen's shoulder and pushed him toward the house. "Catch you in a few!"

Jaylen jostled him back, and although this time their roughhousing seemed playful, Avery narrowed her eyes. There was an almost angry vibe between the two of them that had never existed before. And why would they question meeting in the tree house?

She shook her head. She had to stop stressing.

Walking down the driveway, Avery forced her eyes

away from her former house and focused on the split-level next door to it. The Sernett place, happily, was exactly as she recalled. No cars sat in the driveway, but the attached garage door was open, revealing a drum kit, an amplifier, and a microphone stand. Avery snickered. Hopefully, Paige's older brother, Brandon, had improved as a guitarist. Last summer the neighbors complained his punk band sounded like a pack of screeching hyenas at a construction site.

Reaching the yard, Avery hesitated. The Sernett house appeared deserted. Paige might still be at the mall. She chewed her lip. In years past, she'd never thought twice about letting herself in—Paige's house was like a second home to her. Now she wasn't so sure.

A blur of movement streaked behind the living room picture window, making Avery jump. A second later the front door burst open. Paige, suntanned and long-legged, dashed out, her curly blond ponytail bouncing behind her.

"Yay, yay, yay!" she squealed, barreling down the concrete steps toward Avery.

Avery dumped her bags in the middle of the yard as Paige enveloped her in one of her famous bear hugs. "OMG! You're so tall," Avery said.

"I know, right?" Paige giggled, rocking the two of them back and forth. "I'm almost as tall as Brandon now, which makes him so mad!"

"Wait." Avery pulled away and scrutinized her best friend. "Did you get contacts?"

"Yup." Paige batted her eyelashes. "Just the other day! They are so hard to put in, though!"

"But I thought we were both going to get them at the same time and deal with it together. . . ." Avery's voice trailed off. Paige's eyelashes definitely had mascara on them. And was she wearing lip gloss? That was a new development.

"I know, but my mom had time to take me to the eye doctor last week, and I wanted to surprise you. Besides, now I can show you how to put them in." Footsteps scuffled on the stoop behind Paige. Before Avery could peek around her and identify who was there, Paige pulled her close. "Don't flip out, she's really nice now," she whispered.

"What? Who?" Avery craned around to peer past Paige. Her mouth dropped open.

A petite girl stood there.

Bethany Barnes.

Bethany Barnes, who called Avery four-eyes. Bethany

Barnes, who had bullied Avery for being the only kid at Lincoln Elementary smaller than she was.

Bethany Barnes, Avery's mortal enemy since kindergarten.

"Hi there." Bethany smiled sweetly. The mouthful of bright pink braces she'd had since fourth grade was gone, leaving perfectly straight pearly whites. She wore a plaid skirt and polished black platform loafers, looked cute, and knew it.

Paige scooped Avery's backpack from the ground. "I'm soooo happy you're here, Aves!"

Avery struggled to understand what was happening. Paige, Jaylen, and Tyler had always avoided Bethany out of loyalty to her. So what was her nemesis doing at the Sernetts'? It registered that Bethany held a big paper bag branded with the logo of some expensive clothing store.

"Oh," Avery said slowly. "You two were shopping together."

Bethany stepped down to the yard, snapping her gum. "Yup."

"Camp ended early today," Paige cut in swiftly. "The counselors had a pizza party for us at Sal's, and then, since we were already at the mall—"

"Got it." Avery wiped her suddenly sweaty palms across her ragged jean shorts. Paige had chosen shopping with Bethany Barnes over picking up her best friend at the airport. That stung.

"Plus, Jaylen and Tyler said they'd get you," Paige said.

"How's Philly?" Bethany asked, now at Paige's side.

Avery stiffened. It could be an innocent question. But how much had Paige told Bethany about her new life? "Fine," she said flatly.

"Cool." Bethany rested her hand on Paige's forearm. On her wrist was a purple-and-white friendship bracelet. And circling Paige's wrist was a matching one. Avery's stomach flipped. Bethany continued, "When I get back from Chicago in a few days, we should all hang out. Let's have a slumber party at my house."

"Great," Paige said brightly.

No, no, no. Avery tried to catch Paige's eye, but her best friend only nodded cluelessly.

"Oooooh, my cousin gave me an old Ouija board," Bethany said with a yip of excitement. "We should totally try it out!"

"That would be awesome," Paige said. "Right, Aves?"

Avery blinked at her. Was this a joke? It was one thing for Paige to hang out with Bethany Barnes. They had to talk about that. But that didn't mean that Avery had to spend time with her, too. And since when was Paige into scary stuff? This person was not the best friend she knew.

"Okay, bye!" Not waiting for an answer, Bethany strode across the lawn and down the sidewalk. Avery and Paige watched her go, an awkward silence building between them. Bethany's legs were as tanned as Paige's. Avery glanced down at the peeling skin on her own knees. She pretty much just burned in the sun.

The second Bethany was out of earshot, Paige faced Avery. "I can tell you're mad."

"I'm not mad," Avery lied, even as her shock and pain morphed into anger.

"Well, since Jaylen and Tyler said they'd pick you up—"

"Wow, really?" Avery interrupted. "That's not the problem. Don't you remember in third grade when Bethany told everyone my house smelled like a garbage can?"

"Of course I do." Paige grabbed Avery's hand. "Listen, Bethany and I got put into the same group at gymnastics camp."

"So?" Avery could hardly believe she had to explain why Paige's friendship with Bethany was a huge betrayal.

"I told you, she's different," Paige said. "She apologized for how mean she was to you when we were younger."

Avery wiggled her hand out of Paige's grip. "Well, she didn't apologize to me."

"Give her a chance. Please," Paige begged. "People change."

Avery wavered, but stayed silent. Her best friend had changed, that was for sure. If the past year had taught Avery anything, it was that she *hated* change.

Paige's blue eyes glistened with tears. "I'm really sorry I didn't come get you. I didn't think it'd be a big deal since the boys could do it."

Avery softened. She didn't want to start off her visit on bad terms.

"And we don't have to stay over at Bethany's if you don't want to." Paige grasped Avery's suitcase by the handle. "Let's just concentrate on us."

"Okay, good," said Avery.

But as they walked toward the house, she decided it'd be too risky to give Paige the special friendship bracelet in her backpack at this point. She'd be devastated if Paige didn't put it on right away.

The visit wasn't starting out like Avery had expected.

CHAPTER THREE

TO AVERY'S RELIEF, PAIGE HAD TO PUSH A PILE OF DIRTY clothes into her bedroom closet to make space on the floor for Avery's things. At least one part of her best friend was the same—she still was pretty much a slob.

"I brought the new Lark and Ivy mystery," Avery said, holding out the paperback for Paige's approval. "We can read it together and try to crack the case."

"Hmmm. I guess." Paige leaned against her desk, her thumbs madly texting on her cell phone. Without her glasses, her appearance had totally transformed. She looked much more grown-up and really pretty.

Avery self-consciously straightened her own glasses

on her nose. How she hated having to adjust them constantly. She couldn't wait to get contacts. "You guess?"

"Oh yeah, sure." Paige set her phone on her desk. Avery didn't dare ask who she'd been texting. Because if the answer was Bethany Barnes, it would crush her. Paige flopped onto one of the two twin beds. "Since my parents are gone this weekend, they left money for us to get Barbecue Shack for dinner tonight. Natalie is going to pick it up and bring it back in an hour."

"That's so sweet." Avery's mouth watered. Barbecue Shack was her local favorite.

"Sometimes they're okay," Paige said darkly.

Avery wasn't sure what that meant, but Paige was always dramatic. She brushed it off, eager to see if Paige acted weird about the tree house, like Jaylen and Tyler had. "We're supposed to meet the guys now. At the tree house."

Paige immediately hopped off the bed and turned away to close her closet door. "Sounds good. Let's go." She'd moved too fast for Avery to gauge her expression. She hadn't shut down the idea, though.

Tyler's dad had built the tree house for him a few years back, before he moved out and divorced Tyler's mom. Tyler spent a weekend a month at his dad's apartment in the next town over, though he didn't talk about him much. He and his mom were pretty close, but since she worked full-time, he could often be found next door at Jaylen's, an arrangement that suited everyone just fine.

Avery and Paige left the Sernetts', crossed the quiet street, and made their way along the well-worn path between the boys' houses. On this side of the block, the yards backed up to Crawley Woods, bordered by a tall cedar fence. The tree house perched high in a willow in the far corner of Tyler's backyard, almost completely shielded by leaves. It was the perfect hideaway, the place Avery and her friends had spent so many lazy summer days playing pretend and plotting schemes.

It was where she had felt truly at home.

A rhythmic plunking noise grew louder as they neared the tree. Peering through the branches, Avery suppressed a smile at the sight of the crooked square opening near the tree house door. Tyler's dad had hastily cut out the window after his son complained the place was claustrophobic and needed more light.

Paige swiftly climbed the rickety ladder leaning against the tree trunk and vanished through the doorway. Avery followed, excitement burbling in her chest like fizzy bubbles from a soda. Once the four of them were together, the fun could truly begin.

When Avery's eyes were level with the floor of the tree house, the bubbles went flat.

Tyler sprawled in a lumpy vinyl beanbag chair playing some game on his phone, and Jaylen stood, tossing a tennis ball against the wall. That was normal. What wasn't normal was the dead leaves littering the floor. The rips in the anime posters. The jagged hole in the roof.

The tree house had never been so neglected.

"Hey, Paigey." Jaylen sauntered to her and reached to tweak her ponytail.

Paige lightly slapped his hand away. "Jay! Stop." She ducked her head but smiled.

Tyler glanced up from his phone. "Come on in, Aves."

Avery remained rooted to the steps. "I don't get it. It's like you guys haven't been up here all summer."

No one met her eye or said anything for a moment.

Jaylen resumed throwing the ball. "Yeah, well, Tyler's always gaming."

"Come on. You're the one always shooting hoops with your gym bro friends," Tyler said.

Jaylen ignored him. "And Paige deserted us for her grandparents for a whole month."

"Like you even noticed," Paige shot back. "You're at sports camps all day."

"What about you, Miss Gymnastics?" Tyler's voice had an edge.

"Whoa, whoa, whoa." Avery broke in. "So, you guys haven't been hanging out?"

Again, her friends went quiet. The only sound was the thump of the tennis ball.

Tyler squirmed in the beanbag chair. "We've been busy," he said.

"Plus, you weren't here, Aves," said Jaylen.

"Well, I am now." Avery ascended the last few steps and entered the tree house uncertainly. She'd been so jealous of her friends having fun without her, and they hadn't even been spending time together. In fact, they were bickering.

Avery pulled a battered leather ottoman next to the beanbag and sat, battling the blaring alarm in her head. She took in a relaxing breath. Who cared what the tree house looked like? The four of them were back together, and that was what mattered. "So, what should we do first?"

"Wait," said Tyler, setting aside his phone. "We want to hear about Philadelphia."

"Yeah," Jaylen said. "Tell us about life in a big city."

Avery waffled. The past year she'd chatted with Paige the most. The guys were in the group text chain, but that was mainly filled with jokes and funny videos. Maybe they didn't know how hard moving had been for her. "I don't know. There are a lot of people."

"I wish I lived somewhere with a pro football team." Jaylen sighed. "Or pro basketball or baseball. I'd even take hockey!"

"I heard they have comic cons there." Tyler leaned back, his hands behind his head. "Man, I can't wait to go to one of those."

"I'd go to the art museums," Paige said dreamily. "And the shopping has to be better there."

"You are so lucky, Aves," Jaylen said. "Nothing ever happens in this town. You and your friends are probably never bored."

Avery's cheeks grew hot. She'd told Paige about her trouble making friends, but she didn't want to have to explain it out loud to the guys now. Not in their tree house, of all places.

"Dude." Tyler leaned forward and swatted Jaylen's leg.

"Really?" Paige snatched the tennis ball from Jaylen's hands and dropped it, giving him a pointed look.

"Oh." Jaylen bowed his head. "Sorry. You don't have to talk about that part."

So, Paige *had* filled them in. "It's okay." Avery twirled the friendship bracelet on her wrist. "I mean it's hard, you know? Being the new kid."

"We had a new kid here this year," Tyler said. "Ajay."

"But everyone was nice to him," Paige added.

Of course they were, Avery thought. *Lucky Ajay.*

"He's cool." Jaylen retrieved the tennis ball from the corner where it had rolled. "On Halloween, we went through this new creepy corn maze, Field of Screams, then to Ajay's for a bonfire. His family has this awesome fire pit."

"Great." Avery faked enthusiasm. Had Jaylen forgotten the terrible scar on her arm? Her fingers darted to the bumpy, frog-shaped patch of skin on her left inner elbow. One summer night when she was seven, the Sernetts had hosted a marshmallow roast in their backyard. An ember had burst out of the fire, igniting Avery's sleeve. Before she could stop it, she'd been burned so badly they had to take her to the emergency room. Ever since, a fear of fire haunted her.

As the others droned on about the previous Halloween

and how much fun they'd had, Avery zoned out. She hadn't been invited to any Halloween parties. Instead of having fun, she'd ended up supervising her ten-year-old sister, Julia, and her friends while they trick-or-treated. Unlike Avery, Julia had no trouble fitting in at her new school. Little kids had everything easier.

Paige clapped her hands together, snapping Avery out of her thoughts. "Okay, why are we talking about this? Let's figure out some fun stuff to do now, the four of us. Avery, what's on your wish list?"

Finally. Avery's excitement returned. "Well, we could do the usual. You know, go to the pool. Bike out to Clear Creek."

"Yeah, I guess." Jaylen said, tossing the ball from hand to hand. "But I'm bored with all that stuff."

"Oh. How about miniature golfing?" Avery suggested.

"I've got a new video game," Tyler said. "And I have enough controllers so we can all play togeth—"

"No one wants to sit in your basement." Jaylen whipped the ball at the wall.

Tyler's mellow attitude slipped and his mouth tightened. He quickly recovered. "Whatever," he said carelessly.

"We should definitely go to Penny's on Wednesday night," Paige announced.

"Really?" Avery said. Hanging out in the parking lot of Penny's Desserts eating ice cream on Wednesdays was something older kids did. Wait. She and her friends were going into eighth grade in the fall. Guess *they* were the older kids now.

"Or," Jaylen said, "we should go see *The Séance*."

"Avery won't want to," Paige said.

"What about you?" Avery said. This was ridiculous. She and Paige had always shared their opinion of horror movies. They both hated them.

"It's okay, we'll see it after you go back to Philly." Paige patted Avery's shoulder. "What do *you* want to do, Avery? Really. Anything you want."

Avery debated with herself. Her friends had already squelched most of her ideas. But she'd dreamt about goofing around with Paige, Jaylen, and Tyler for so long, reliving the good old days. She cleared her throat. "How about we play some of the old games?"

"Which games?" A tiny crease appeared between Paige's eyes.

"Like Ridge Road Detective Club."

A split second after the words were out, Avery wished them back into her mouth. Her friends' faces froze, then shifted into disappointment.

"Well . . ." Tyler awkwardly jiggled his knee up and down.

Paige toyed with her friendship bracelet—the one Bethany had given her. "Aren't we a little old for that?"

"Yeah, I mean, I know you just turned thirteen last month," Jaylen said. "But the rest of us will be fourteen in the fall."

Avery wanted to crawl into a hole and hide but managed to choke out a laugh. "I'm joking, guys!"

"Okay, phew!" Tyler said. "Yeah, what were we going to do, spy on Mr. and Mrs. Redmond?"

The Redmonds were the oldest couple on the block. All summer they lounged on their screened-in side porch, drinking iced tea, smoking cigarettes—*blech*—and keeping a strict eye on the neighborhood happenings.

Paige giggled. "Remember that time we hid in their bushes for hours, hoping to hear something good, and all they did was argue about politics?"

"That was the worst!" said Jaylen.

"We were such weird little kids," Tyler chimed in. "How about when we thought Bigfoot lived in Crawley Woods?"

As the others poked fun at their former selves, tears

stung Avery's eyes. What was happening? The tree house was a wreck, Jaylen had turned into a gym bro, Tyler had gotten obsessed with gaming, and Paige wore makeup and liked *Bethany Barnes.* It was as though Avery had landed in a world of fun house mirrors—everything was *almost* like what she remembered but distorted and wrong.

She was losing them. Her best friends. Avery was the one who moved away, but they were the ones who had moved on. They were on the road to growing up and forgetting all the fun they'd had together. She had to keep up with them or be left behind in their dust.

An image of the dusty We Remember sign popped into her mind. Along with a bold idea.

"I know," Avery blurted. "We do one last Detective Club mission, but with a twist. Way more daring."

Jaylen caught the ball on the fly and didn't throw it again. "Go on."

Avery hesitated. The anticipation on her friends' faces was so much better than the cringe they'd tried to hide minutes ago. Adrenaline swooshed through her. "We sneak over to the Old Winter Playhouse tonight and have a *real* séance. We talk to Maddie's ghost."

For a moment, nobody reacted and her words hung in the air. Had she gone too far? Although, that could be a good thing. Paige may pretend to like horror movies, but no way would she agree to possibly facing a *real* ghost. Paige would be the one to say no, and Avery would score points for her daring plan. Then no one could accuse her of being babyish.

"Whoa." A spark lit in Tyler's eyes. "I'll play Detective Club again if we do *that*!"

"Aw, our little rule-follower is breaking down barriers, acting all brave!" Jaylen tossed the ball high into the air before catching it smoothly. "Good for you, Aves!"

Uh-oh. Avery's gaze flew to Paige.

Paige tilted her head. "Isn't there a fence around the building?"

Whew. Avery was saved. "Right," she said, pretending disappointment. "I didn't think of that. Oh well."

"So?" Jaylen shrugged. "We climb the fence."

Avery's insides contracted.

"But the doors and windows are boarded up," Tyler said.

"Duh, ghosts can go through walls, dude." Jaylen threw the ball at him. Tyler bobbled it but saved it from hitting the floor. "We'll just set up right outside the building."

"Hmmmm." Paige tapped her chin thoughtfully. Avery held her breath, waiting for the verdict. A slow smile spread across Paige's face. "I love this idea!"

Avery swallowed. This séance was going to happen. But as her friends' enthusiasm swept through the tree house, a rush of warmth enveloped her. She'd won them back and was part of the group once more. Her hesitation melted away.

She and her friends would be sneaking out.

At night.

To go to an abandoned theater.

To talk to an *actual* ghost.

It sure wouldn't be one of their usual Detective Club missions.

CHAPTER FOUR

AVERY HAD TEED UP THE IDEA, BUT IT WAS THE OTHER three who drove it home.

"We'll do it tonight," Jaylen announced. They were standing in his driveway, about to go their separate ways for dinner. "Me and Tyler can camp out in my backyard, like we used to."

"Yeah, your parents are zonked by ten thirty." Tyler nodded. "No one will check on us after that." He and Jaylen high-fived.

Avery watched them with satisfaction. She still had her doubts about the séance, but at least the guys were already getting along better.

"Ooooh, and my parents are out of town," Paige said. "I know just how to get around Natalie."

"How?" Jaylen raised an eyebrow.

"That's for me to know and you to find out," Paige said smugly.

Locusts buzzed their late-summer song from the tree-tops like a warning. Avery shuffled her feet uncomfortably. She hadn't really thought this through. "Guys, are we sure we want to sneak out? Maybe we should do it during the day?"

Jaylen guffawed. "Ghosts don't come out during the day."

"But, I mean, won't we get in trouble?" Avery had a sudden image of her mom dragging her back to Philadelphia before her visit was over.

"How will anyone know?" Jaylen said.

"Yeah, we won't be gone that long," Paige agreed.

Jaylen stuck out his chest. "Plus, I know I'm not supposed to sneak out of the house, but no one's ever said anything about sneaking out of the yard."

"Right?" Tyler said. "Technically, we're good."

"Later," Paige said. She slung her arm, the one sporting the purple-and-white friendship bracelet, around

Avery's shoulder. Together they crossed the street, their strides falling into perfect sync, despite the difference in their heights. Avery tingled with happiness.

This is going to be great, she told herself. She was back in with her friends, ready for an adventure. There wasn't much she could do to stop it now, anyway. The scheme had taken on a life of its own.

Dinner at the Sernett kitchen table with Natalie and Brandon brought back a ton of good memories. Avery had always admired Natalie, who effortlessly got straight A's and still had time to captain the field hockey team. Sure, Brandon could be annoying, but he had taught Avery to ride a bike, spending hours with her on the trail by the creek and never complaining. She was completely comfortable among them, as if they were her own older siblings.

Halfway through the delicious meal of barbecued pork sliders, corn bread, and mac 'n' cheese, Paige nudged Avery.

"Hey, Nat." Paige casually wiped barbecue sauce off her hands with a paper napkin. "Bethany Barnes invited Avery and me to spend the night tonight."

Avery's appetite shriveled away. This lying thing was hard for her. Jaylen was right: she always followed the rules. It had to do with being a firstborn child, or at least that's what her dad had told her. Jaylen and Paige, both the youngest in their families, were the rebels. Tyler was an only child, so technically he was a firstborn, too, but he wasn't as rigid as Avery.

Brandon, pimply and wearing a constant scowl that was new to Avery, slurped his lemonade noisily.

Paige glared at him. "You're so gross."

Brandon burped in response.

Natalie dropped her fork, full of potato salad, to her plate. "Please stop it. There's been too much arguing around here lately."

Paige lowered her head sheepishly.

"Sorry, Nat," Brandon said.

Avery crossed her fingers under the table, willing Natalie to say no. Then the séance would be canceled and it wouldn't be her fault.

"Well . . ." Natalie fiddled thoughtfully with one of the half-dozen silver earrings in her left ear. "You've stayed at Bethany's before, right?"

"Oh yeah, lots of times," Paige said. Avery winced. Hadn't Paige said they'd only started hanging out this summer at gymnastics camp? Paige went on. "Mom knows her."

Natalie shrugged. "Okay, fine by me."

Avery deflated.

"Excellent," Brandon said through a mouthful of cole-slaw. "I have cross-country practice at six a.m. tomorrow, and I don't need you two keeping me up all night with your obnoxious giggling."

"Whatever," said Paige. She winked at Avery.

In Paige's room after dinner, the girls searched on their phones: *how to do a séance.* As they scrolled through the websites, phrases like "spirits can be malicious" and "do not be manipulated by evil" leapt out at Avery.

She laughed uncomfortably, trying to act carefree. "You sure we should be doing this?"

"Heck yeah!" Paige continued searching. "Oooooh, Bethany is going to be so jealous when she finds out she missed this!"

Avery shut down her doubts. This séance was her way to prove to Paige that she was just as cool as, if not cooler than, Bethany Barnes. Plus, it had been too long since she'd done anything fun.

She and Paige made a scene of pretending to pack their backpacks for a sleepover. Paige called loudly to Natalie as they left the house, telling her they'd walk to Bethany's. Instead, once the girls reached the end of the block, they doubled back to Tyler's tree house to hide out until midnight.

Before Avery knew it, dusk had fallen. They watched one of their favorite movies on an iPad to make the time go faster, a goofy comedy about a summer camp, and they giggled together like they were eleven years old again. But all too soon the credits rolled, the movie was finished, and Avery's uncertainty resurfaced.

"Do you ever wish you could go back to when we were little?" Avery perched on the beanbag chair and drew her knees to her chin.

Next to her on the ottoman, Paige sipped from her water bottle. "Not really. I mean, we had fun, but I can't wait to grow up. You know." She set the bottle on the floor. "Over the last year, I've been craving more adventure. To have more freedom, like Nat and Brandon."

"Right." Avery nodded, playing along.

"I'm so glad you came up with this séance idea, Aves," Paige said. "To be honest, I was kinda worried about your visit."

There it was. Avery couldn't hide the pain that flitted across her face, though she masked it as fast as she could.

"Don't get me wrong," Paige said, rushing to fill the

silence. "I was *so* excited to see you. But I've really grown up this past year. I wasn't sure we had that much in common anymore."

"Oh," Avery said as neutrally as possible. "I get it."

Paige stretched out her long legs and touched her toes. "Like, those Lark and Ivy books seem a little . . ." She stopped her thought. "Well, I barely have time for reading anymore. I've got swim team and choir and homework. And I love going to high school football and basketball games on weekends. You know?"

Avery didn't know. She'd tried art club at her new school and hadn't bonded with anyone there. She couldn't find a swim team to join and didn't have a friend to go to high school games with. So she spent all her free time reading. In fact, she took comfort in rereading the old books from years ago, when she and Paige would go to the library together all the time.

Hoo, hoo.

The unexpected sound floated into the tree house. Startled, the girls locked eyes. Then they cracked up. Avery's heartache eased. She crawled to the door of the tree house and poked her head out. Jaylen, dressed in black clothes and carrying a backpack, waited on the grass below.

"That was the worst owl impression I've ever heard," Avery whispered.

Jaylen's grin couldn't be missed in the light of the full moon glowing over the houses. "But it worked."

"Shhhh," Tyler said, sneaking around the tree trunk. He, too, wore black from head to toe. "Quiet until we're in the woods."

"Yeah, then I'll fill you in on what Russell told me," Jaylen whispered.

"About what?" Avery asked.

"Just wait," Jaylen promised.

Avery grabbed her backpack full of séance supplies. Paige stashed the iPad in her bag and shoved it into a corner behind the ottoman, as they'd planned. She drank the rest of the water from her bottle.

"No use taking this," she said, chucking it on the floor next to her bag. "Ready?"

"Ready," Avery said.

They descended the ladder. The adventure had begun.

The most direct way to the Old Winter Playhouse was through Crawley Woods (or Creepy-Crawley Woods, as Jaylen called them). Over the years, the kids had often explored its running paths, fallen trees, and burbling creek, but always during the day and usually with at least one older sibling nearby. This trip would be a different story. The thought of tromping through the woods late at night triggered a deep anxiety in Avery, but she knew they couldn't risk anyone spotting them on the streets after midnight.

The group followed the wooden fence through several backyards until they got to the Redmonds' section. As usual, that gate was unlocked.

The light of the moon barely penetrated the thick umbrella of leaves, making the woods unrecognizable.

"Can we use our cell lights?" Avery asked. "Or is that too risky?"

"Maybe just one of us can, and the rest can follow," Tyler said.

"I should go first," Jaylen said, switching on his light.

"Why?" Tyler challenged him.

"I have a great sense of direction." Jaylen charged ahead.

Tyler puffed out an annoyed breath and Paige nudged him. "Let him do it," she said. "It's not like we'll get lost. We can always use the maps on our phones if we need to." She plunged into the woods after Jaylen.

"Fine," Tyler mumbled.

They fell into a single-file line snaking through the

shadowy trees, their feet crunching on dead leaves. Tree frogs croaked. Mysterious shapes rustled through the undergrowth. The temperature had dropped even more—surprising for an August night. Luckily, at the last minute, Avery had thrown on a thin hoodie over her tank top and shorts.

She gingerly picked her way along the path, striving to avoid tripping on tree roots. If she twisted her ankle and hurt herself, they would have to turn back. Avery stopped short. Maybe she should fake a bad fall and pretend to be injured. Then the séance would have to be canceled.

No. Her friends would see right through her. She'd never been much of an actor.

Ahead, Tyler paused and turned around. "Coming?"

"Yes." Avery hustled to catch up.

When she reached his side, Tyler poked her arm. "Nervous?"

Avery shook her head. "Seriously? How can you tell?"

"I know you." He playfully squeezed her shoulder. "It'll be fine. Nothing's going to happen, anyway. I don't believe in ghosts."

Avery peered up at him. He'd grown more inches than even Paige had. "Then why are you doing this?"

"I don't want to be left behind," Tyler admitted. "And this is a great way to kick off your visit, right? One last Detective Club mission. The four of us, like old times." A wistful note crept into his voice.

Avery searched his profile, but it was too dark to read what he was thinking. Maybe he didn't like how their friendships were changing, either. "Ty—"

"Guys, quit stalling and get up here," Jaylen called. "Time for some ghost stories."

"What does that mean?" Avery said under her breath.

Tyler picked up his pace. "Since Laila won't tell him anything, he called Russell to get the scoop on the ghost."

"Oh." A spooky story was the last thing Avery needed to hear while sneaking through Creepy-Crawley Woods after midnight. She didn't really have a choice, though.

When she and Tyler caught up to the others, Jaylen rubbed his palms together.

"Get ready for terror!" he said in a scratchy voice.

"Me first!" said Paige as they continued along the path. "Brandon and his friends said once that Duke Olsen's cousin heard piano music coming from inside the theater late one night. Even though it was all boarded up! And a little girl's voice singing 'Rock-a-Bye Baby.'"

A gust of wind jostled the trees.

Tyler snorted. "I don't believe it. What was Duke Olsen's cousin doing there late at night, anyway?"

"I don't know," Paige said defensively. "That's just what I heard."

"That's it?" Jaylen said. "Okay, time for my story."

Avery braced herself.

Jaylen faced them, walking backward and miraculously not veering off the path. "Okay, Russell told me high schoolers used to sneak into the theater with a case of beer. Which was fine if they stayed in the lobby, or away from the auditorium. But the second anyone stepped onto the stage, they'd feel invisible hands grabbing their ankles, trying to pull them away."

Tyler made a small noise in his throat. Skepticism rolled off him in waves.

Jaylen ignored him. "So, one Halloween, during a full moon like tonight, a group of people dared each other to walk across the stage. When they did, a mysterious sound came out of nowhere."

Paige squealed with delight. "What was it?"

"It was a little kid giggling."

An animal skittered across their path, its eyes glowing. "Whoa!" Avery leapt back.

"It's just a raccoon, Aves," Jaylen said. "Geez, you're jumpy."

"Go on!" Paige said.

Jaylen continued. "Then this one guy, Frankie Smith, got to the middle of the stage. Suddenly, Maddie's ghost dove at him from the catwalk, moaning 'You'll die, too!' Everybody there witnessed it. And they all took off, but Frankie tripped and fell. And no one realized he'd been left behind until they were in the woods."

"No!" Paige said breathlessly.

"Yup." Jaylen lowered his voice. "Frankie finally escaped, but he never told anyone what had happened while he was alone in the theater with the ghost. And he was never the same after that. In fact, he completely stopped talking. Part of his hair went white. His family had to move away."

"That sounds made up," scoffed Tyler. "When was this?"

"What am I, a reporter?" Jaylen shot back. "Anyway, the owners of the theater heard the story. That's when they put up the fence, according to Russell. But people still heard and saw the strange things late at night. Finally, the owners put in the ghost light. And it must work, 'cause no one has seen the ghost since."

A black shape swooped down on them from the trees.

Paige gasped and Avery yelped. Whatever it was flapped away into the night.

Jaylen snickered. "Perfect timing."

"Just a bat," Tyler said matter-of-factly.

That didn't make Avery feel any better. "Let's change the subject," she said. "How high is this catwalk?"

"Pretty high, I think," Tyler said. "They used it to hang lights and equipment above the stage."

"Does anyone know why Maddie went up there?" Paige asked.

"Nope. Obviously, she wasn't supposed to," Tyler said. "According to my mom, the cast were all sitting in the auditorium talking with the director, and then . . . Maddie fell."

Avery winced. It felt wrong to be making a fun adventure out of a tragedy. Out of a kid's *death*. She had a flashback to second grade, when a boy in her and Tyler's class, Alejandro Martinez, had died of leukemia. One time Bethany Barnes had lied to Mr. Gallagher in art class, claiming Avery had pinched her, and Alejandro had stuck up for Avery. He'd told the truth, that because Avery had been mixing paints across the room, there was no way she could've touched Bethany. Alejandro's older brothers and sisters had been so sad when he was put in the hospital. The Martinez family had moved away after he died, just like Maddie's family had.

The wind abruptly picked up, forcing Avery out of her head and into her body. She wrapped her arms around herself against the chill. They'd been wandering the woods way too long.

The running path took a sharp turn, but instead of following it, Jaylen plowed straight ahead. The trees thinned, allowing wispy rays of moonlight to penetrate the darkness. They stepped out of the woods.

"Guys, we're here," Jaylen said, switching off his light.

CHAPTER FIVE

ON THE OTHER SIDE OF A SMALL, GRASSY FIELD LOOMED the back of the Old Winter Playhouse. To its right was the empty parking lot lit by a single, flickering security light on a high pole. Beyond the building, the road stretched, deserted and silent. Avery had an attack of the jitters.

The kids crossed the field, the trees of Crawley Woods creaking behind them in the wind. Above them, clouds slunk across the full moon. They stopped at the chain-link fence. In the middle of the brick wall on the other side were two large metal doors, beige paint chips hanging off in hunks, a padlocked chain connecting both handles. A small security camera dangled from a wire above the doors, its glass lens cracked and pointed at the ground. To the left was a smaller door spray-painted with graffiti.

TURN BACK, Avery read. Her jitters increased.

She meekly tapped the fence. "Um, how are we climbing over this thing without impaling ourselves?"

"Never fear, I'm a genius." Jaylen dug into his backpack, beaming, and pulled out a beach towel.

"Yeah, but you're not tall enough to implement the plan." Tyler wrested the towel away from him and draped it along the top of the seven-foot fence, covering the sharp metal tips that jabbed up into the night air.

Jaylen's grin evaporated. Without hesitation, he aggressively scaled the fence, making it shake and clang, then dropped to the other side. "I'm doing a perimeter check."

Tyler followed, easily swinging his long legs over the fence. "I'd better go, too."

"You don't have to," Jaylen grumbled.

"What are you checking for?" asked Paige.

"Maybe there is a way into the building." Jaylen rattled the locked double doors while Tyler tried the smaller entrance. Neither had luck opening them. They jogged toward the parking lot, each pushing to get ahead of the other.

"Be careful!" Paige called as they disappeared around the corner of the building.

"What is going on with them?" Avery asked. "They've been picking on each other all day."

Paige shrugged. "They're getting more like Brandon. Competitive and grouchy. Natalie says all teenage boys are like that."

Avery had her doubts. The beef between Jaylen and Tyler seemed more personal to her. Then again, she didn't have a brother, so what did she know? Teenage boys were pretty much a mystery to her.

Paige, nimble from gymnastics, had no problem climbing the fence. Avery, though, struggled to get a toehold. Her cheeks burned from embarrassment. She was nowhere near as graceful as Paige.

"Here, toss me your backpack." Paige held up her hand. Avery awkwardly heaved her backpack over the fence. Paige caught it easily and reached out her other arm. "I got you."

"No, I'm good." Avery rammed one sneaker into an open link, gripped the fence above her head, and willed her way up. It took forever, and she had trouble getting over the top, but she eventually succeeded. She landed on the dirty cement with a smack and lost her balance, almost careening into Paige.

Paige steadied her, but Avery shrugged her off and seized her backpack. "It's too bright back here for a séance 'cause of the parking lot light," she babbled, trying to cover up her humiliation. "Come on."

Before Paige could answer, Avery bolted in the opposite direction the boys had gone. Why, oh why, was she so awkward? When had Paige gotten so graceful?

And why was she comparing herself to her best friend? She'd never done that before.

At the end of the wall and around the corner, Avery found a weedy side yard. Though the full moon still shone, the building blocked the parking lot light. A line of pine trees hid the road.

"You're right, this is better," Paige said, coming up behind Avery. She snapped the beach towel. "We can sit on this."

Two shadowy figures emerged from around the front of the playhouse.

"Stop talking about us," Jaylen called.

"Did they hear us?" Avery whispered guiltily.

"He's just kidding," Paige said.

Avery frowned. She'd always found Jaylen so easy to read before. He'd gotten so sarcastic since last summer it was hard for her to tell when he was joking.

"There's no way in." Jaylen had acquired a stick and scraped it along the building's brick foundation as he strolled toward them. "Everything is locked or boarded up."

"We saw one more security camera," Tyler added, "but it was all busted, too. So we're good. No one will know we're here."

The scraping sound from Jaylen's stick abruptly changed tone, like the point had grazed a different type of surface. "Hold up." He stopped about two-thirds of the way along the wall. Using the stick, he pushed aside a patch of scraggly weeds. "There's a window here!"

Paige scurried over to investigate. Avery plodded behind her apprehensively. Tyler shone his cell light on a warped board attached to a window frame by rusty nails. A section of wood in an upper corner had rotted away, leaving a small hole. Jaylen jabbed the stick at it. The board toppled from the wall with a swoosh, flattening the weeds and revealing a window without a pane.

"Whoops," Jaylen said.

A cold, musty draft seeped from the basement, chilling Avery's bare legs. "What'd you do that for?"

"I barely touched it. The wood's all rotten." Jaylen squatted low to get a closer look.

The rest of them bent over, straining to see inside the building. The light fell on some cardboard boxes, a bookshelf jammed with knickknacks, and a large black trunk.

"Must've been a storage room for props and stuff," Tyler said.

"Put the board back," Avery whispered.

"Why?" said Jaylen. "This is like an invitation."

"Like the ghost wants us to come in," Paige said with a mischievous smile.

Jaylen plopped onto the ground and dangled his legs inside the building. "We came this far, might as well check it out." In one swift movement, he slid out of sight, his backpack bumping on the window frame behind him. There was a thud and a grunt.

"Jaylen! Are you okay?" Avery called. If he got hurt down there, they'd have to get help, and then they'd be busted.

"Sheesh, I'm fine." A beam of light began moving

below. Jaylen had turned on his cell light. He whistled. "You guys, this is soooo cool. There is the weirdest stuff down here."

"Like what?" Tyler asked.

"Come and check it out," Jaylen said. He cackled like a witch. "Unless you don't have the guts, Ty-Ty."

"Fine." Tyler, usually so laid back, rapidly lowered himself onto the edge of the window frame. "I'm going in." He was gone before Avery could pull him back.

As Paige surged forward, Avery snagged her arm, stopping her. "I don't know about this," she said.

"It's not like we're breaking in. They should've secured the building better. That board was just waiting to fall off." Paige gently escaped Avery's grasp. She slung the towel around her neck, her eyes sparkling in the moonlight. "We came here for adventure, right?"

"Whoa, is that a suit of armor?" Tyler exclaimed from below.

Jaylen cracked up. "It's wearing a cowboy hat!"

"Wait for me!" Paige scooted onto the edge of the window frame and vanished inside the building.

"But . . ." Avery couldn't believe her friends had gone in without thinking of any consequences. "How are you guys going to get out of there?"

"Easy, Aves," Jaylen called. "We'll pile up some of this junk and climb out. Hold up, is that a *sword?*"

"Wow! Check out these weird hats," Paige said.

Avery paced the weeds. She was missing out on all the fun. Again.

Snatches of whispers floated up to her.

". . . scared . . ."

"Whatever . . ."

". . . leave her."

"You really don't have to come down." Paige flitted back into Avery's line of sight, her body only a black silhouette below. "It's fine if you stay up there and wait for us. Just give us your backpack with the candles and stuff if you do." She twirled away from the window.

That was it. No way was Avery going to be left behind. She plunked onto the sill and let herself fall into the darkness.

For the second time that night, she didn't stick the landing. When her sneakers hit the floor, she tumbled over, bashing her knees on the rough cement.

"You good?" Tyler was at her side.

"I'm fine," Avery said through gritted teeth. She quickly pushed to her feet and switched on her cell light to discover what she'd gotten herself into.

They were in a long room running along the side of the building and filled with all sorts of odds and ends. Beyond the boxes, tall shelves loaded with everything from books to picture frames to plates and glasses lined the walls. Rolled-up rugs rested in a heap in front of a couple of old-fashioned, overstuffed chairs. Sure enough, a suit of armor wearing a cowboy hat commanded the middle of the room.

Clammy, mildewy air invaded Avery's nose and crept over her skin. She shivered. Next to her squatted a low black trunk, its lid halfway raised. Inside were a bunch of Thanksgiving-like Puritan hats, a Boston Red Sox pennant, some feather pens, and a small black pot.

"Weird," she muttered.

Paige was examining a freestanding clothes rack. "Ooooh, costumes!" She unzipped a garment bag. Immediately wings whirred and a stream of moths whooshed into her face. She frantically swatted them away. "Gross!"

The moths continued in a straight line up and out the window.

Avery swept her light in an arc. When the beam touched the room's far corner, she froze.

A man lurked there, utterly still, his head angled grotesquely down to his shoulder.

CHAPTER SIX

"OH MY GOD!" AVERY SCRABBLED BACKWARD, CRASHING into a stack of paint cans.

"What?" Paige pivoted and aimed her light at the corner.

It illuminated a mannequin with a broken neck.

"Oh!" Avery's heart raced. "I thought . . ."

"Everyone needs to chill," Tyler said.

"Wonder where this goes." Jaylen had found a door in the wall across from the window. He pulled it open. Beyond was a narrow space, possibly a hallway, facing another closed door. Light filtered in from somewhere to the left. "You guys, there are stairs. And a light's up there."

"The ghost light?" Tyler asked.

"Probably." Jaylen held open the heavy metal door with his foot. "Come on! Let's go."

"Really?" Avery twisted her fingers in the backpack strap at her shoulder. She still hadn't recovered from the shocking sight of the creepy mannequin in the corner. Why had she suggested this again?

"Uh, yeah!" Jaylen bobbed his head. "I can't think of a better place to have a séance than the actual spot where the kid died."

"Makes sense," Paige agreed.

Avery balked. "When you say it like that, I don't know. Isn't this kind of . . . disrespectful?"

"This was your idea!" Jaylen argued.

True. Avery bit her tongue. Still, this mission was starting to feel ghoulish to her.

"Fine, let's vote," Tyler said. "Raise your hand if you want to go on the stage."

Jaylen thrust his arm into the air. Tyler followed suit, and Paige lifted her hand. They all turned to Avery.

"Just wait here, Aves," Paige said, edging toward the door, a hint of impatience in her tone.

"Yeah, I'll take your backpack." Tyler held out his hand.

As hesitant as Avery was, she was sick of being left behind. "No way. We should stick together."

They filed out of the room, Avery last to leave. As she stepped into a small hallway, she caught the door with her elbow right before it swung closed behind her. "Tyler! Help me prop this open, just in case."

"Good idea," he said.

Tyler held the door while Avery fetched a ladder-backed chair from the jumble of furniture in the storage room. She hurriedly stuck the chair in the opening between the door and the jamb as Jaylen and Paige charged up a staircase and Tyler took off after them. The door thumped into the chair and stopped, creating a gap. Satisfied, Avery sped after her friends.

At the top of the stairs, they found themselves in a small nook with a tall stool and a podium. To the left, a series of ropes and pulleys scaled a brick wall. A black box similar to Brandon's guitar amplifier sat to one side. The atmosphere was stiflingly stale.

"Okay, we're backstage in the wings," Tyler said.

"Thank you, Captain Obvious," Jaylen said.

Paige tapped the black box. "My dad got a fog machine like this last year for Halloween."

Jaylen zeroed in on a low table that held a collection of wicked-looking weapons and grabbed a short dagger. "Check it out!"

"Careful!" said Paige.

"It's fake." Jaylen thrust it at her, and she yelped before dissolving into a fit of giggles.

Avery ducked out of Jaylen's reach and between two parallel black curtains that formed a short tunnel leading to the stage. She stepped free of the curtains, aimed her light forward, and faltered. "Whoa."

Three gravestones stood in front of her. Her friends crowded behind her.

"Bruh," Jaylen cracked. "For a minute I thought they must've buried Maddie here."

Paige gave him a push. "This is the set for the play, silly."

"What the heck kind of play takes place in a cemetery?" Jaylen asked.

"A Halloween one?" Tyler offered.

Something about the set tickled a memory in Avery, but she couldn't quite place it. "Why is everything still here?" she asked.

"I'm not sure," Tyler said.

Despite the layer of dust, the stage appeared suspended in time, as if the actors could return any second for their curtain call. A coffin-sized hole was cut into the floor in front of the center tombstone. Avery cautiously stepped closer. Beyond a tangle of spiderwebs, the hole was about three feet deep, its bottom a wooden platform, its sides open to the blackness beneath the stage. A prop shovel lay on the floor nearby, next to a canvas drop cloth like the ones painters used to protect the floor from paint drips. A tattered gray curtain covered the back wall.

At the edge of the stage rose the ghost light, a floor lamp consisting of a single light bulb surrounded by a metal cage atop a pole about as tall as Avery. A bright yellow extension cord ran from its base into the wings on the opposite side of the stage. Beyond the ghost light rows of red velvet seats spread into gloom.

Avery glanced up, beyond the arch that framed the stage and hid the lights and rigging from the audience. Far above, a skinny iron bridge with a waist-high railing spanned from one side of the stage to the other.

A catwalk.

"Wait," Paige whispered. "She fell from way up there?"

Avery instinctively shifted her gaze to the floorboards

under the catwalk. They all did. Jaylen picked up the drop cloth and peered underneath it.

"I don't see any blood," he said matter-of-factly. He let the drop cloth fall and, realizing everyone was staring at him, shrugged. "What? We were all thinking it."

No one said a word. The theater was eerily quiet. It was, Avery thought, like the building itself was a tomb, and they were all buried inside it.

She hitched up her backpack. "We're really doing this, right?"

"Yeah, let's get it over with," Paige said, for the first time giving off a nervous vibe.

"Great." Tyler pointed to the area in front of the hole in the stage. "Let's set up here."

Avery made herself busy, pulling out supplies from her backpack and concentrating on reassuring thoughts. She was with her best friends, the séance would be fun, there was no such thing as ghosts. She set three pillar candles on the floorboards and handed the long-stemmed butane lighter at Paige. No way was Avery going to play with fire right now. She was shaky enough as it was.

"Now," Paige said. "To summon a spirit, we need to sit in a circle with our knees touching and the candles in the middle."

Jaylen maneuvered himself next to Paige and Tyler took her other side, so Avery ended up across from her. They settled on the floorboards and sat cross-legged. Avery's scraped knee smarted when it bumped up against Tyler's leg.

Paige had to click the lighter a bunch of times before a weak flame spit out. Right away, the scar on Avery's elbow throbbed. She purposefully breathed slowly, attempting to stay calm. Paige successfully lit one candle, but then the lighter quit working. She shook it forcefully.

"It's out of fluid," she said, dropping it on the floor.

"Way to be prepared," Jaylen teased. "Did you even test that thing before you brought it?"

"Shush." Paige picked up the lit candle and used it to ignite the other candles' wicks.

"Guys, shouldn't we turn off the ghost light if we want to talk to a ghost?" Jaylen asked.

Avery bit the inside of her cheek. She'd secretly hoped that everyone would forget about the ghost light. Then its beam would protect them, the séance would fail, and there'd be no way anything spooky would happen. Or, at least, less of a chance. As Tyler had said, a ghost light could just be part of a silly superstition.

"Facts." Tyler sprang to his feet and groped around the pole until he found a switch at the base of the bulb. "Ready?"

Avery's eyes found Paige's. Paige gave her a confident smile and nodded.

Jaylen impatiently drummed his fingertips on his legs. "Let's gooooo."

Tyler flipped the switch, plunging the stage into near darkness except for the feeble illumination from the candles. He rejoined the circle.

"We need to hold hands, too," Paige said.

They grasped hands, Jaylen smirking. Avery tried to recall the last time she'd held hands with Jaylen or Tyler. Probably in first grade. She squirmed inwardly.

Paige closed her eyes. "Maddie, hello. We're here to speak with you. We mean no harm."

Jaylen snickered.

"Stop it," Paige hissed. "I'm just doing what the website said to."

The candles cast ghastly shadows from under their chins, turning everyone into scarier versions of themselves—Tyler's nose sharper, Paige's eyelashes spidery, Jaylen's gap-toothed grin like a jack-o-lantern's. Avery's palms grew damp with sweat. Beyond their circle, scraps of tape glowed in several spots on the floorboards. The gravestones were ominous lumps.

"Hello, Maddie?" Paige said. "Please, speak with us."

Pause.

"Let us know you're here."

"Whooooo."

Avery stiffened. Tyler sighed. Jaylen's eyes widened innocently, even as the sound emitted from his barely open mouth.

"Would you cut it out?" Paige kicked him slightly with her foot.

"Ouch!" said Jaylen.

A faint, hollow whistle came from above.

Avery tightened her grip on Tyler's hand. "Do you hear that?"

They all craned their heads up. Without the ghost light, the grid that made the bottom of the catwalk was barely visible. Beyond it, far up in the roof, was a gray, square outline.

The whistle returned, louder this time, echoing eerily around the space.

"I think there's a vent in the ceiling," Tyler said. "That's moonlight coming in."

"So, it's the wind making that sound?" Avery's voice wobbled.

"Yeah," said Tyler. "It's actually good there's a vent, or this place would be even stuffier."

"Shhhh," Paige said. "Maddie, we would love to speak with you. Are you here?"

The only answer was another feeble rush of wind.

Jaylen fidgeted. "This isn't working."

"Maybe everyone should close their eyes, not just me," said Paige. Avery watched as everyone else did, then closed her own. Paige cleared her throat. "Maddie, we are only here to say hello."

Silence.

"Please show yourself."

Nothing.

"Maddie?"

Avery opened an eyelid. Paige was frowning, her eyes screwed shut. Tyler was clearly peeking out from under his lashes, and Jaylen was blatantly watching Paige.

Paige's eyes popped open, her gaze catching Jaylen mid-stare. "Jaylen, do you want this to work or not?"

"Fine," Jalen huffed. He closed his eyes.

Avery did, too.

Paige resumed speaking. "Maddie, are you here?"

There was no answer.

"I told you there wasn't a ghost," Tyler said under his breath.

The tension Avery had held in every muscle of her body since she'd suggested the séance eased. "I mean, that would be good, right? If Maddie has passed on. Better than hanging around here."

"Come on, guys, let's keep trying," Paige ordered. "We came all this way. Let's all take a deep breath."

They did.

"Maddie, are you here?"

A candle sizzled.

"Maddie," Paige continued, "no one has forgotten your story."

"We're sorry this happened to you," Avery added impulsively. A soft breeze brushed her cheek. *Just the air from the vent,* she thought.

Abruptly the wind chilled and increased, swirling around her. Avery's eyes snapped open. Tyler had gone even paler, his freckles standing out in stark contrast to his white face. Beyond the wildly flickering candle flames, Paige's ponytail whipped across her cheeks. What was happening? Jaylen squeezed Avery's hand and jerked his chin toward the ceiling.

Avery followed his gaze, her mouth going dry. The

figure of a young girl paced the catwalk. She wore shorts and a T-shirt, her hair was a fluff of curls—she looked like any other kid, except for the sickly, gray-green glow that radiated from her skin. Back and forth she stalked, hands covering her ears, mouth forming words that were indecipherable over the rising wind.

"Maddie?" Paige squeaked.

The ghost abruptly stopped, slapped its palms on the railing, and pushed itself up until its feet dangled above the catwalk floor. It leaned over, eyes bulging toward the back of the stage, totally unaware of the séance directly below.

"I'm not afraid of heights!" it howled, violently shaking its head from side to side. "I'm not!"

"Oh no," said Avery with a terrible, creeping realization. "No!"

The ghost's body lurched forward, and for a moment it dangled on the railing, torso hanging in open space, legs still over the catwalk. Its mouth opened, and a high, thin wail built above the roar of the wind. Then it toppled over the railing, falling straight toward the séance circle. Avery caught a spark of recognition in the ghost's eyes, as though it saw them sitting there before its mouth spread impossibly wide and obliterated the rest of its face.

The candles went out.

CHAPTER SEVEN

AVERY THREW HER ARMS UP TO PROTECT HERSELF, BUT NO impact came. The wind cut off, the ghost vanished, and her friends erupted in chaos.

"Go, go, go!" yelled Paige.

In the pitch black, Avery scrambled to her knees, cracking heads with Jaylen, who was doing the same thing. She fumbled for her backpack and clambered upright, almost falling flat as her feet tangled with the towel.

"I can't see!"

"Turn on your light!"

Hands shaking, Avery pulled her cell from her pocket and jabbed at it uselessly.

Tyler got his light on first. "Come on!"

They staggered in a clump toward the wings, Tyler leading, Avery right behind him.

"Quick!"

"Don't push!"

Someone knocked into something that crashed to the floor with an earsplitting clatter.

"Watch it!"

They thundered down the stairs. As the jiggling beam of Tyler's light hit the chair propping open the storage room door, Avery caught her breath. The gap leading into the storage room had shrunk to a sliver, and the chair was halfway over the threshold. Before Tyler could reach it, the weight of the door finished pushing the chair into the hall.

BANG! It slammed shut.

"No!" Tyler shouted.

"What happened?" Paige gasped.

"Open it!" Jaylen demanded.

Tyler bumbled over the chair, grasped the door handle, and turned. "It's locked!"

"What?" Jaylen shoved Tyler aside. He twisted the handle and threw his shoulder against the door.

It didn't budge.

"Is it after us?" Avery panted, clutching her backpack to her chest.

They backed against the walls, straining to see if anything chased them. The space at the top of the stairs was dark and silent.

Paige's teeth chattered with fear. "What was it doing? Reenacting her death or something?"

"Maybe," Jaylen said. "That happens on those ghost hunter shows."

"Those shows are fake," Tyler said, shaking his head.

"Really, man?" Jaylen snapped. "You gonna say that after what just happened?"

Tyler backpedaled. "Okay, there was definitely *something* unexplained—"

"I'll explain it," Jaylen said. "Ghosts are real, and we saw one. Boom."

They all stared at each other, wild-eyed.

Jaylen broke into an impish grin. "And I can't wait to tell everyone."

"But how are we going to do that?" Paige said in a panic. "We're trapped!"

"There has to be another way out," Tyler said.

Avery edged slightly to her left. She'd been leaning on the closed door across from the storage room.

"This must go under the stage. Maybe there's another window?"

"Yes! Let's go!" Paige exclaimed.

Avery twisted the doorknob. To her relief, the door opened. A waft of foul air smacked her in the face. Something squeaked and scuttled in the darkness beyond.

Paige gagged. "Shut it!"

Avery slammed the door. "What was that smell?"

"Something dead," Tyler said. "Probably mice."

"That was way too loud to be mice," Paige said. "That had to be rats."

Jaylen's eyes bugged out. "Do *not* say that. I hate rats."

"But we might have to go in there," Avery said. "That could be the only way out."

"No, actually, we don't." Jaylen's face lit up. "There was no other basement window. We checked the perimeter, remember?"

"Are you sure?" Paige asked Tyler. He nodded tensely.

"Oh right," Jaylen said, his face sagging. "Guess I shouldn't be happy there isn't another window."

Avery's stomach dropped as the reality of the situation sank in. What if they were trapped? "So how are we getting out of here?"

Tyler held up his phone. "We'll call someone for help."

"Nooooo," Jaylen groaned. "I'll get in so much trouble."

"Me too," Paige said. "And after I get in trouble, Natalie will murder me for getting her into trouble."

Avery's eyebrows flew up in disbelief. "Guys, who cares about getting into trouble? We're stuck in here with an actual ghost!"

Tyler glanced up from his phone. "I don't have service. Does anyone?"

Avery checked. She had no bars. Her friends' dejected expressions told her they didn't, either.

"Seriously?" Paige slumped against the wall.

"Probably because we're in a basement," Avery said. "So that means . . ."

Their heads all swiveled toward the steps. Tyler aimed his light at the top of the staircase. The space remained a black hole.

"I'm not going up there again," Paige said.

"We have to," Tyler said. "We can't stay down here. It's too cramped, anyway." He pulled on the neck of his T-shirt, like it was too tight against his skin.

Avery swiped a hand across her sweaty forehead. "Okay. It's okay. We're going to get out."

"I know." Tyler snapped his fingers. "We'll turn the ghost light back on."

"I thought you said that was a superstition," Jaylen said sarcastically.

"The ghost didn't show up until we turned it off, so maybe it does work," Tyler said.

"Oh, so now you believe?" Jaylen crossed his arms.

Tyler grimaced. "It can't hurt."

"But—but . . . ," Paige stuttered.

Jaylen placed his hand reassuringly on her shoulder. "I'll protect you, Paige."

Tyler clenched his jaw. "Really?"

The motionless air in the hall stirred, and the temperature dropped.

"You guys feel that?" Avery whispered.

Beyond the staircase, in the hallway's dead-end shadows, something shifted. Goose bumps stung Avery's skin as an icy breeze rose to a howling wind. A gray-green, glowing mass grew and pulsed until Maddie's ghost materialized. Its mouth jerked stiffly like a marionette's, or like it hadn't been used in a very long time. Its eyes glared.

"GET OUT!" it screeched.

Avery hurtled headlong into the freezing wind and up the stairs, her friends pushing at her heels. At the top she almost tripped over the fallen podium, but Jaylen grabbed her elbow, righting her, and they all careened between the black curtains and onto the stage.

"Turn on the ghost light!" yelled Tyler, shining his light on it from behind.

Avery dashed to the pole, the wind continuing to pour from the basement. She fumbled for the switch and flipped it. The light blazed on.

The wind ceased. They all whirled to face the wings. A big bright dot from the sudden light blocked Avery's vision. It slowly cleared, revealing only the fallen podium. No ghost.

"Where'd it go?" Paige squeaked.

"I don't know," Avery said. The catwalk above their heads was empty. Far beyond in the ceiling, the square of moonlight around the vent gleamed faintly. The absence of the howling wind amplified their ragged breathing.

Tyler checked his phone. "I still don't have service."

"Me neither," said Paige, a hint of hysteria pushing her voice unnaturally high.

Avery and Jaylen each looked at their screens and shook their heads. He crammed his phone into his shorts pocket and kicked listlessly at the ghost light pole.

"Why is the ghost so mad, anyway?" Jaylen asked. "We didn't do anything to it."

"Maybe because we interrupted its rest," Paige said, wrapping her arms around her body as if to give herself a comforting hug.

While Tyler prowled the floorboards, holding his phone above his head to try to get service, Avery assessed the stage. Where their séance circle had been, the beach towel was a crumpled heap, the candles toppled over and scattered. Jaylen's backpack had somehow ended up hanging at the precipice of the grave, on the verge of tumbling into the hole. She zeroed in on a damaged spot on the yellow extension cord, a few feet away from the base of the ghost light. The cord's bright plastic covering had been gnawed away, exposing the interior wires. Avery couldn't help imagining the light fizzling out, the ghost charging, its awful mouth stretching wide . . .

She turned to alert her friends about the mangled cord, then pressed her lips together. No use reminding Jaylen about the rats. He'd get too worked up.

"Guys." Tyler had stopped roaming and was fixated on the floor behind the middle tombstone.

"What?" In three strides, Jaylen stepped next to him. He sucked in a breath. "What the . . . ?"

Avery and Paige shared an uneasy glance. Together, they tentatively circled the grave.

At the base of the tombstone lay a human skull.

Paige gasped. "Seriously?"

Avery shuddered. Brown splotches stained the skull, a nasty crack spread above its left eye socket, and its teeth were jagged and crooked. It taunted them with a hollow sneer.

"That thing is real," Jaylen said.

"How do you know?" Tyler challenged. "Have you ever seen a real skull?"

"No, but I've seen fake ones, and this sure doesn't look fake." Jaylen jabbed it with the toe of his sneaker. The skull toppled onto its side.

"Don't touch it!" Avery said.

"Why would they have a real skull here?" Tyler rolled his eyes.

"How would I know that?" Jaylen scowled. "Ask your mom."

They were picking on each other again. Avery couldn't stand it. "Hey, the theater is a concrete box," she announced. "Of course we don't get reception. Let's get out of here and try the lobby."

"Solid plan," Tyler said.

"But what if the ghost is out there?" Paige whispered. "She wants us gone."

Jaylen tipped his head back. "Hey, Maddie!" he called to the rafters. "We are trying to leave, okay? So give us a break."

"Don't bother her again!" Paige's eyes were huge.

"What?" Jaylen said. "She needs to know we're doing our best to get out of here, like she wants us to."

"She doesn't seem very reasonable," Tyler muttered.

Avery felt dizzy. If they ventured into the lobby, they'd be away from the safety of the ghost light. But they had no other choice. "Okay. Who wants to go first?"

"I will," Jaylen said, full of bravado. He swiped his backpack from the edge of the grave and strolled downstage. Tyler sniffed with disapproval.

Avery stuffed the beach towel and the two candles she could find in her own backpack. In one front corner of the stage, a narrow set of risers led to the auditorium floor. As she descended, the wood creaked and shifted unsteadily. She braced her hand on the plaster wall next to her. The last thing she wanted to do was fall into the deep orchestra pit on the other side. Then she'd crack her head on the upright piano or bash into the jumble of folding chairs and music stands, she was sure of it. She was thrilled to reach the auditorium's sticky concrete floor.

The four of them crept along the upward sloping side aisle, each shining their own light around the space. They passed row after row of red velvet upholstered seats, some ripped open, gray stuffing bulging like blisters. Avery's sneakers crunched on broken bits of white plaster. Swinging her light to the ceiling, she glimpsed several chunks missing.

Great, she thought. *The roof could cave in.*

"Check out these paintings." Tyler pointed at the side wall. Old-fashioned frescos depicted prairie landscapes, river bluffs, and wild horses running free.

Avery did a double take and squinted at the horses. All of their eyes were eerily white, as if rolled back into their heads in terror.

In the beam of their phone lights, dust motes speckled the air like tiny snowflakes.

"I feel like I'm on one of those ghost hunter shows." Paige giggled uncomfortably. "If an orb comes at us, I'm really going to lose it."

A bead of sweat trickled down Avery's back. "What's an orb?"

"Like, a glowing, floating ball of spiritual presence," Jaylen explained.

A new thing to worry about. Avery bit her lip.

Above the main floor, there was a balcony with a half-dozen rows of seats. As they passed under it, the atmosphere grew stuffier and Avery's breaths shallower. Was it even safe to breathe ten-year-old air? Although it wasn't like she had a choice.

The back of her neck prickled with the feeling of being watched. She twirled around.

To her surprise, the arch above the stage featured carved cherubs and even a smirking gargoyle or two, a head broken off here, half a foot missing there. The ghost light kept watch, its illumination touching the tombstones and shovel but not reaching into the deep shadows of the wings. Just visible behind the center tombstone, the skull lay motionless on its side. Its sightless black eye sockets drilled a hole through Avery.

She shuddered and scurried to rejoin her friends. They'd reached a set of double doors in the rear wall of the auditorium.

"Okay, let's go." Tyler pushed down the bar across the

right door. It broke away from the left door with a sticky snap and squealed open. Avery aimed her cell light past his shoulder.

Paige screamed.

Floating in front of them was a glowing skull.

CHAPTER EIGHT

"NO!" TYLER JUMPED BACK, CRUNCHING AVERY'S FOOT.
The lobby door swung free and smashed into her elbow.

"We have to go back!" Paige squeaked.

"Wait." Avery shoved the door wider with her aching funny bone and aimed her light at the skull. "It's fine."

Her beam illuminated a black poster board leaning on an easel. At the top, red letters spelled out:

The Midnight Players present

Hamlet

A play by William Shakespeare

Below was a lifelike illustration of a skull.

Jaylen snickered. "Big man, Tyler."

"Like you weren't just as scared as me," Tyler retorted.

Paige clapped her hand to her forehead. "Guys, stop!"

"This explains the graveyard," Avery said. "I should've known. My mom teaches a class on Shakespeare. She made me watch a *Hamlet* movie once."

"You?" Jaylen joked. "Watched a movie with graves and skulls?"

"There's a ghost, too. And murder." Avery had pretended to pay attention but secretly just messed around on her phone. Mom had busted her and hadn't been happy. "Yeah, it wasn't my favorite story."

They ventured into the two-story lobby. Red-and-black patterned carpet covered the floor. Several low leather benches lined the walls. A broom leaned against a display case that held theater memorabilia—past play programs, shellacked newspaper clips, even an arrangement of old props. Directly ahead, glass double doors reflected the bright circles of their roaming cell lights, but plywood on the other side blocked any view of the outside world. High above, a series of windows were also boarded up, though cracks in the wood allowed moonlight to seep through.

"Does anybody have reception?" Tyler asked.

They each checked their screens and shook their heads.

"Can we turn on some lights?" Paige asked.

"Here." Jaylen reached next to the door they'd come through a moment before and flipped a row of switches. Nothing happened.

"Okay, there has to be electricity," Paige said, balling her hands into fists. "The ghost light works."

"I still say phones are our last resort." Jaylen strutted to the glass doors and rattled them. They didn't open. "Let's break the glass, then kick out the boards."

"Um, how?" Avery pictured glass flying. She glanced at Paige, who freaked out at the smallest paper cut and hated blood. By the petrified expression on Paige's face, Avery knew she was thinking the same thing. "We do not want to get cut."

"Then get out of the way." Jaylen swaggered to a bench and shrugged off his backpack. "Tyler, help me ram the doors."

"This is dumb," Tyler said. "It's probably shatter-proof glass."

"So we shouldn't even try? Do you want to get out of here, or what?" Jaylen lifted one end of the bench and positioned it perpendicular to the doors.

"Fine." Tyler got on the opposite side from Jaylen, and together, they picked up the bench. Avery and Paige scooted out of the way.

Jaylen nodded. "One. Two. Three."

They clumsily took off toward the door and struck the glass. The door shook but held fast, the bench bouncing back and throwing them off balance. They dropped the bench.

"I told you that wasn't going to work," Tyler huffed.

In one swift motion, Jaylen raised his leg and slammed the bottom of his sneaker into the glass.

"Jaylen!" Paige shouted.

Again, the door held.

Jaylen hopped backward on his other leg and cradled his foot. "I had to try."

Avery stepped closer to the door and examined it. "Um, there's a keyhole. Let's try to find the key." She shone her light at one end of the lobby, where it landed on a half door, the top open and the bottom closed. A sign above read Coat Check. Metal hangers gleamed in the darkness beyond. She swung her light to the opposite end of the lobby. There, an open window yawned above a short counter displaying a Tickets placard. Next to it, a hallway led into even more darkness. "Any ideas?"

No one made a move. Tyler opened his mouth, as if he had something to say, then snapped it closed. Jaylen picked up his backpack, avoiding Avery's eyes. His confidence had clearly taken a hit after his failure to break down the door. Paige's lips pressed together in a thin, tense line. Now that the stakes were higher and physical danger threated them, her enthusiasm for adventure had evaporated.

"Well, this is silly," Avery blurted, surprising herself by taking charge. "There's probably an office. That would be where I would keep a key."

She marched toward the hall, passing a fallen poster board featuring a dozen black-and-white actor photos, names printed below their chins. Her friends trailed behind her.

In the hall, an open doorway led to a large room with filing cabinets and a couple metal desks. A small flicker of accomplishment warmed Avery from inside. She'd found the office. "Let's find that key."

Like the stage and despite the dust, the office seemed ready and waiting for people to clock in and pick up their work where they left off. The desk closest to the door held stacks of papers and a vase of flowers so dead, a weak breeze could turn them into dust. A plastic trash can lay on its side, garbage spilling out next to a small refrigerator. A calendar from ten years prior hung on the wall under a clock with both hands pointing straight up.

Stuck at midnight, of course. The witching hour. Avery battled a rising sense of dread.

Jaylen flipped the light switch. "Of course it doesn't work," he moaned.

"Why is it like this?" Paige asked. "Like, nobody emptied out this place anywhere. They just . . . left."

"I think there's still a lawsuit or something from Maddie's family," Tyler said. "So, they are leaving stuff as is? I don't know."

"There's a phone." Jaylen pointed at the far desk, where an ancient-looking cordless landline. "I guess I could call Laila to come get us. If I promise to do her chores for the next year, maybe she won't tattle." He forced a grin.

Tyler darted to the phone, seized the handset from its base, and lifted it to his ear. His shoulders drooped. "It's dead."

Dead. The word reverberated through Avery's mind.

Jaylen was already rifling through desk drawers. Avery tackled the desktop, shuffling papers aside, peeking under a keyboard left behind without its monitor, dumping the contents from a coffee mug acting as a pencil holder. No keys. She picked up a framed picture. Two teenagers with mouths full of braces beamed at her. She hoped their teeth were straight now, ten years later.

Paige opened the small refrigerator. The brown, shriveled remains of an apple rolled out. "Ewwww."

Jaylen banged a drawer closed. "Nothing."

A cardboard box labeled Lost and Found rested in a corner. Avery knelt next to it and rummaged inside, finding a sweatshirt embroidered with a college logo, a broken umbrella, and a small red purse. She eagerly unzipped the purse. It contained only a pack of cigarettes. Nothing useful.

They all searched for several minutes more and came up empty-handed.

Paige lifted her heavy ponytail and fanned the nape of her neck with a notebook. "It's really stuffy in here."

"And it stinks." Jaylen wrinkled his nose.

"There's one more place to check." Avery pushed open a door that led into the rear of the ticket booth. A long counter under the window held a couple of binders and another landline. She listlessly picked up the phone handset, not hopeful at all.

Hissing static filled her ear. She sucked in a breath. "Guys! I think this phone works!"

There was a flurry of excitement from the office. Paige and Jaylen crowded into the ticket booth. Tyler lingered in the doorway.

"Hello?" Avery said into the mouthpiece. The static increased, forcing her to move the phone away from her ear.

Paige inched closer. "Hello? We're trapped in the Old Winter Playhouse! We need help!"

The static stuttered to a stop. They all waited breathlessly.

A droning whisper began, babbling incoherent syllables.

"Hello?" Avery said uncertainly, still holding out the phone.

"We need help!" Paige repeated.

The line crackled.

"You shouldn't be here," hissed a high, giggling voice.

"Wha . . ." Avery locked eyes with Paige, confused.

"You shouldn't be here, but you are!" The voice snickered. "So, let's play let's play let's play let's play—"

Avery dropped the phone and it crashed onto the

counter, the voice ranting on, louder and louder. Paige covered her ears and backed into Tyler as Jaylen scooped up the handset, stabbed the off button, and threw the phone to the floor.

The sudden quiet was deafening. Avery legs wobbled. Even Jaylen's eyes were wide with horror.

"Was—was that the ghost?" Paige said.

"And . . ." Avery's voice trembled. "What does that mean, it wants to play?"

The phone rang.

Without hesitation, they all dashed out of the ticket booth, through the office, and into the lobby. Behind them, the ringing abruptly cut off. Tyler, in the lead, halted and flung out his arms, blocking the others from moving.

"Wait, listen!"

"What?" Paige panted.

"Exactly!" Tyler said. "It—"

A cacophony of sounds exploded—wind chimes, a booming bass line, an old-fashioned car horn, a croaking frog. Avery panicked, until she recognized the frog croak came from her own phone. A notification was coming through. They were all getting one.

They fumbled with their phones as the racket continued without a break. Three dots pulsed in the lower left corner of Avery's screen. "I'm getting a text!" she said.

Paige gaped at her cell. "Me too!"

"Maybe our families have figured out we're gone," Tyler yelled over the din.

"Yeah, but . . ." Jaylen examined his screen. "Mine says 'unknown sender.'"

"Wait, how can we get notifications before a text comes through?" Paige was freaking.

"I don't know." Avery's throat went dry. "And I still don't have service."

The sounds stopped, leaving an eerie hush. The dots vanished from Avery's screen.

"Whoever it was isn't texting anymore," Jaylen said.

"Here, too," Paige said, holding up her phone.

"This is good news, guys," Tyler said, his positivity making a comeback. "Our phones aren't completely inoperable."

"I hate to break this to you, Tech Bro, but it's one thirty in the morning," Jaylen said. "Our families did not just all text us at the same time."

Tyler's face fell. "Okay, but . . ."

"And you guys," Avery said, her stomach knotting. "My phone is on silent mode."

"Mine, too," Jaylen said apprehensively.

"What is happening?" Paige clamped a hand to her mouth.

Something clanged behind Avery once. Twice. Again and again.

The noise crescendoed into a deafening clatter. Avery whipped around and shone her light into the coat check. The beam glinted off the empty hangers as they danced madly on the rods, bashing together by some invisible force.

"The ghost!" Avery said.

Paige gripped her arm. "We gotta get back to the light!"

They fled into the auditorium where it had all begun.

CHAPTER NINE

THE FOUR OF THEM TORE DOWN THE AISLE AND UP THE
steps to the stage, practically climbing over one another
in a frenzied race to reach the ghost light. When they
got there, they clung to the pole like it was their last
defense, the only weapon that could save them.

Only then did Avery dare peek at the rear of the auditorium, convinced the hangers were ready to shoot at
them out of the gloom. Fortunately, only the dust motes
churned through the air, disturbed by the kids' frantic
rush through the theater.

"Are we safe now?" Paige was out of breath.

"We'd better be," Jaylen said, for once not clowning
around. A new sheen of sweat glistened on his forehead.

He cupped his hand to his mouth and raised his head toward the catwalk. "Hey, Maddie, we're trapped, okay? Give us a break."

"Stop talking to her!" Paige whacked his arm. "That's what made her come out in the first place."

Jaylen scowled. "Says the person who kept begging her to talk."

"How was I supposed to know she'd get so mad?" Paige said.

"Let's stay calm," Tyler broke in.

Paige turned on him. "You keep saying that, but it's hard to be calm with a ghost on the loose."

"A ghost who wants to 'play,'" Avery added. "Whatever that means."

"I don't think it's talking about Monopoly," Jaylen said.

Avery shuddered. "What if she's hiding in the shadows, watching us?"

"If?" Paige sputtered. "Of course she is!"

"All right then, let's get rid of the shadows," Tyler said matter-of-factly. He regarded the large stage lights hanging above them. "Like you said, Paige, the ghost light works. So one of those should, too, right?"

"You'd think," Jaylen muttered, one eye on the skull.

"There's gotta be a control box backstage," Tyler said.

"How about over there?" Paige pointed into the wings opposite from where the basement staircase was. "Let's go check it out. I need to do something! I'm not going to sit around here waiting for her—it—to attack."

She grabbed Tyler's hand and pulled him toward the unexplored side of the stage. He stumbled along behind her. Jaylen, now laser-focused on the skull, ignored them. Avery stayed put. If Jaylen wasn't going anywhere, she wasn't, either. She couldn't leave him alone.

Who are you fooling, Avery? The truth was, she was too chicken to leave the ghost light. The creepy voice on the phone still rang in her ears. She shakily unzipped her backpack, got out her water bottle, and took a swig. It barely dampened her parched throat. If only Paige hadn't finished all her own water back at the treehouse.

Jaylen edged closer to the skull. "Is that thing in the same place I left it?"

"What?" Avery choked on her water. When they'd left the auditorium, the skull had been glaring directly at her. Somehow it still did, even though she now faced it from a completely different angle. It must have rotated. But how? She wiped her hand across her mouth. Maybe skulls were like the subjects in portrait paintings—the eyes always followed you, no matter where you moved. That had to be it.

Still, a heavy blanket of dread settled over her.

"You guys!" Paige called. "We found a bunch of switches and a fuse box!"

A series of clicks came from offstage. Avery crossed her fingers and eagerly watched the lights above. But they remained dark.

Jaylen squatted next to the skull, tilting his head to be at the same angle it was. "This thing is totally real. Tyler doesn't know what he's talking about."

The ghost light flickered. Avery nervously eyed the damaged cord. If that light gave out, they'd be in huge trouble.

Jaylen picked up the skull and lifted it close to his face.

Suddenly the light died and the world went completely black. Muffled exclamations erupted offstage. An icy wind slithered around Avery.

Something breathed in her ear. "Get—"

Snap! The ghost light flashed on. The wind evaporated. Avery spun around, temporarily blinded. Who was behind her?

"Sorry, sorry, sorry!" Paige called. "Some of the

switches are labeled, but most of them are too faded to read." The clicking started again.

Avery blinked rapidly, searching the stage. There was no sign of the ghost. Jaylen, still locked in a staring contest with the skull, acted unbothered. But the chills running up and down her body couldn't be denied. It must have been the ghost whispering to her.

"J-Jay . . . Did you hear that?"

"Huh?" Jaylen shook himself out of his trance and lowered the skull away from his face. "Oh, yeah. Paige flipped the wrong switch."

"No, I mean . . ." Avery wavered. Was her mind playing tricks on her?

Paige and Tyler shuffled out from the wings.

"Nothing works," Paige said dejectedly.

The skull slipped from Jaylen's grasp and dropped to the floor with a dull thud. He lumbered upright and backed away from it, wiping his hands on his shorts. "Why is it slimy?"

"Ewww, why did you touch it?" Pagie said.

Avery had had enough. "You know what?" She charged to the drop cloth, picked it up, and tossed it over the skull. "I can't stand that thing staring at me."

Tyler scratched the back of his head. "It could be

that the fuses are blown. We might find another electrical box in the basement—"

"No!" Jaylen yelled. He flung his palms up. "No, no, no! I'm not going down there with the rats."

They all stared at him in astonishment. He heaved in big gulps of air, as if he'd just come off the basketball court. Avery stepped toward him and touched his arm lightly. "That's all right, we won't make you."

"More lights don't really matter right now," Tyler said. "We should concentrate on getting out of here."

Paige hugged herself. "True."

"Everyone, check your battery power," Tyler said. "What percent are you at?"

Avery fished her cell out of her back pocket. "Fifty-three."

"I'm at forty-four," said Paige.

"Seventy-nine," Tyler said.

Jaylen squinted out at the auditorium, his face troubled.

Avery nudged him. "Hello?"

"What? Oh." He glanced at his screen. "Three percent."

"Seriously?" Paige said.

Tyler's mouth twisted with disapproval. "Dude, you never keep your phone charged."

"I will from now on," Jaylen said. "If we ever get out of here."

Paige pushed him. "Stop joking."

He didn't respond.

Avery had a flash of inspiration. "Okay, hold on. Maybe we can get cell reception higher up in the building."

Tyler's eyes lit up. "We did find a ladder attached to the wall in the wings. It goes to—"

"Not the catwalk!" Paige said in alarm.

"No," Avery reassured her. "There's a window in the back wall above the balcony. I think it's part of a control room for the lights and the microphones and stuff. If we go up there, maybe our phone will work."

"And we can try to turn on more lights," Tyler added.

"Do we have to get there through the lobby?" Jaylen toyed with one of his braids. "'Cause I don't want to run into the ghost again."

"There's probably a way up there from the stage, too," Tyler said, gearing into action. "Let's see where that door by the podium leads. My phone has the most power, so let's use my light. Everyone else turn their phone off."

"Good idea," Paige said.

Avery shouldered her backpack, and they all tromped

to the podium side of the stage. She slowed before passing the staircase. What if the ghost lingered down there? It could fly right at her, its mouth spreading wider and wider, its wind pinning her to the wall so she couldn't escape. . . .

Knowing it was silly, she held her breath, like she did whenever traveling past a graveyard. Supposedly that prevented spirits from possessing your body. Avery scurried past the stairs and made it to the podium without anything horrible happening. Behind her, Jaylen also inhaled deeply and increased his pace.

Guess she wasn't the only superstitious one.

The door beyond the podium opened to yet another hall with several doors, this one running from the back to the front of the building. At the closest end was the small exterior door Tyler had tried to open after hopping the fence.

"This is like the high school's haunted house at Halloween," Paige whispered. "All hallways and closed doors and who knows what behind them."

"Did you have to say that, Paige?" Avery envisioned a bloody inmate in an orange jumpsuit leaping out at them with a chainsaw. A mad professor wielding a knife. A crazed clown yowling with laughter.

Or the ghost of a disturbed young girl ambushing them, mouth jerking as a shriek ripped from her throat—

"Let's go." Tyler's words cut through Avery's nightmarish thoughts. He headed toward the lobby.

The first door in the middle of the hall was actually ajar. Tyler paused in front of it. "Here we go."

He pushed it open and leapt back, aiming his cell inside like a stunted lightsaber. Its beam landed on a low counter lined with two rows of severed heads.

Avery stifled a scream.

Tyler passed through the doorway. "This must be the dressing room."

"But . . ." Avery's voice trailed off. What had appeared to be severed heads was only a row of wig stands displayed in front of a makeup mirror. She adjusted her glasses on her nose. Either she needed a new prescription, or she couldn't trust her own eyes.

Or she needed to get a grip.

Avery entered the room. To the right was a sink, some lockers, and two plaid couches. An open door to the left led to a toilet with no water in its bowl.

Tyler nodded toward the bathroom. "Anybody have to go?"

"I've sweated all the liquid out of my body," Jaylen said.

"Gross." Avery elbowed him, assuming he was joking. But his face was stony.

Paige patted the couch cushions. "I guess we could sleep in here, if we had to."

"I mean, we could," Jaylen said. "But it would just be prolonging the inevitable."

Paige flinched. "What's that supposed to mean?"

"Let's stick with the plan," Tyler said. "We need to get upstairs."

They left the dressing room and continued along the hall, Jaylen lagging behind. Tyler cautiously cracked open the next door, revealing a stairwell with steps going up to the second floor.

"Bingo," he said.

"Hold up." Jaylen's eyes darted around the hallway. "Do you hear that?"

"What?" Paige asked. They all froze and listened.

"That, like, scratching." Jaylen's face was tight with horror.

Avery's blood ran cold. She listened, but all she could hear was her heart pounding in her ears.

"No," said Tyler.

"Are you sure? It sounds like rats." Jaylen rubbed his arms like he was freezing cold.

"Dude, quit thinking about the rats." Tyler ran a hand through his hair impatiently. "Rats don't attack people out of nowhere."

"They do if they're hungry enough." Jaylen's voice rose. "What do they have to eat here besides us?"

"What is going on with you?" Avery had never seen Jaylen so rattled. It was one thing for her to worry—that was normal. But sunny Jaylen acting frightened and defeated? That was almost more troubling to her than a ghost.

Jaylen backed away from the group. "You know what? I'm not going up there. I'm staying with the light." He turned and retreated down the hall, shoulders hunched under his backpack.

"No, we have to stay together." Avery lunged to grab his shirt, but he dodged her and continued toward the stage door.

"I'll go with him," Paige said. "Jaylen! Wait for me."

He paused, shifting from one foot to the other like he was eager to make a break for it.

"I don't think splitting up is a good plan," Tyler said under his breath.

Paige handed Avery her phone. "Take this and check it for service up there."

"What about Jaylen's phone?" Avery asked.

"His is about to die, anyway," Paige said. "We all have the same carrier. If ours don't work, his won't, either. We'll only turn his light on if we need it, so we won't waste the battery."

As much as Avery longed to return to the ghost light, too, Paige had a point. No one should be alone. Plus, the way Jaylen was acting, he wouldn't be any help anyway. "Let them go," she said to Tyler.

"Fine," he huffed.

Paige jogged to Jaylen and linked arms with him. He immediately pulled her toward the stage door. Avery waited until they'd entered the wings, then turned to Tyler.

"Ready?" she asked.

Scowling, he spun on his heel and pushed open the stairwell door. To Avery's relief, nothing jumped out at them. As soon as she passed the threshold, the door banged shut behind her, enclosing them inside.

Avery hadn't imagined the building's air quality could get any nastier, but she'd been wrong. The stairwell's cement walls oozed moisture, and the mildew stink threatened to choke her.

Tyler kicked the lowest stair before stepping on it. "What is up with Jaylen?"

"Right?" Avery stuffed both her phone and Paige's in her backpack's outer pocket before trailing Tyler and his light up the staircase.

"One minute he's showing off for Paige, the next he's freaking out," Tyler grumbled. "Ever since those two kissed, he's—"

Avery stopped so hard her sneaker made an ear-splitting squeak, the echo rebounding around the stair-well. "WHAT?"

CHAPTER TEN

"OH." TYLER FROZE, ONE FOOT ON A STEP, THE OTHER ON
the landing. He shot Avery a guilty look. "Paige didn't
tell you?"

"No." Avery's mind reeled. In second grade, the four
of them had spied on the older kids playing spin the
bottle and witnessed Paige's sister, Natalie, kissing Jaylen's brother, Russell. The Ridge Road Detective Club
members had been beyond disgusted. They'd made a pact
then and there to always be friends and never, ever anything more. Because anything more would be gross. "I
can't believe it."

"Well, it's true." Tyler leaned his back against the
wall and bowed his head.

"When was this?" Avery asked.

"At the beginning of the summer," he said darkly.

"Were you there? I mean, was it a dare or something?" Avery remained locked in place, her hands gripping the railings. This was even bigger than the Bethany Barnes betrayal. How many secrets was Paige keeping from her?

"No, I was not there. And it absolutely was not a dare." Tyler laughed bitterly. "I'm a poet and I didn't know it."

"So, what happened?"

Even though his cell light pointed toward the floor, Avery could see Tyler's jaw clenching. "I was at my dad's," he said. "So the two of them biked to get ice cream after dinner one night and stopped in Autumn Park on the way home. They were sitting next to each other on the swings and . . . they kissed."

"But why?" Avery couldn't wrap her mind around it. "Do they like each other *that* way?"

Tyler shrugged. "He likes her. I don't know what she thinks. I guess it only happened once."

This was huge. Avery trudged up the steps and joined him on the landing. She'd never kissed anyone in a romantic way. There was a boy at her new school, Joe Doyle, who gave her butterflies when she passed him in the hall. He'd smiled at her and said hi once and her insides had gone so squishy she thought she'd collapse on the spot. She'd totally told Paige about him. In the past, the two of them had dreamt together about their first kisses, who they'd be with, what they'd be like. It was absolutely inconceivable that Paige hadn't told her about this.

Jaylen would've been Paige's first kiss. At least as far as she knew, Jaylen would've been Paige's first kiss.

Bethany Barnes probably knew for sure.

Tyler traced a circle on the ground with the tip of his shoe, still not meeting her eyes. "Listen, I don't know anything else, so if you want more facts, you'll have to talk to Paige."

"Wait." Something clicked in Avery's mind. Tyler was almost more upset about this kiss than she was. "You like her, too, don't you? In *that* way."

"No," Tyler said quickly. Too quickly.

"Tyler." She put her hands on her hips.

"Okay. Kinda." He finally raised his head. "I mean . . . yeah."

Avery's hands dropped to her sides. She had never thought of Jaylen and Tyler in a romantic way. They were like brothers to her. Sometimes she even hated them, though that never lasted. She absolutely didn't want to kiss either of them, ever. Still, she felt a pinprick of jealousy. Should she be insulted that the boys didn't think of *her* that way? Paige triumphs again. She twisted the bracelet on her wrist. Since when had she gotten so competitive with her best friend?

"Does Paige know you like her?" Avery asked.

"No!" Tyler jolted like he'd stuck his hand in an electric socket. "I hope not! Please, don't tell her." His eyes were pleading. "I mean, if she doesn't like me back—"

"Right." Avery totally understood. It was hard to put yourself out there unless there was no question the other person was interested in you, too, whether you wanted to kiss them or just hang out and be friends. She'd learned that at her new school. "How about Jaylen? Does he know?"

"Absolutely not," Tyler said emphatically. "No way was I gonna tell him that after I found out they kissed."

More secrets. Avery had never thought there would be so many between her friends. This changed everything. The way the boys had been fighting made much more sense now. "So that's why you've been picking on him."

"Have I?" Tyler shrank back, surprised.

"Are you kidding? Totally. And Jaylen might not know why, but he's noticed, too, believe me. Things have been tense between you two the whole time I've been here."

Tyler groaned. "You're right. I hate it."

"Now I get why you haven't been in the tree house much, either."

"Well, that, and it's true, we've all been busy. Plus, Jaylen's been hanging out with guys from sports camp lately and acting tough." Tyler cracked his knuckles. "That's not really my thing."

Avery processed this. Tyler and Jaylen had been inseparable since preschool. She'd never ever dreamt they'd be at odds. Everything she believed about her friends had turned upside down in the last twelve hours.

Tyler straightened. "But what can I do? I can't stop Jaylen from trying new stuff. And things change."

"I wish they didn't," Avery said.

Tyler pushed away from the wall. "Forget it. I can't deal with this right now. We have bigger problems." He dashed up the next half flight of stairs.

He was right. Avery hastily went after him.

Tyler had already opened the door at the top. Luckily, no killer clown awaited them. Only another hall with two more closed doors.

"Great, more haunted house fun." Avery tried to be light, but her joke fell flat.

Tyler checked his cell screen, all business. "Nothing yet. You?"

Avery pulled the two phones from her backpack. "Nope."

"Okay." He moved into the hall and clasped the doorknob on the right. "This probably goes to the balcony. Ready?"

"Yes." Avery steeled herself for what might be there.

Tyler eased open the door, peeked inside, then pulled it wide. Ahead, the rows of red velvet seats extended to a wall opposite that held a similar door, probably to another hall. To the right, the rows sloped down to a low wall. On the stage below, Paige and Jaylen huddled together under the ghost light. His discarded backpack lay near the open grave. He hugged his knees to his chest and swiveled his head from side to side, as if he was searching for something.

Paige shielded her eyes with her hand and peered up at the balcony. "Is that you guys?" Her voice sounded tiny in the large space.

"Yes, just us," Avery answered. At this level, the

decorative details above the stage were clearer. The cherubs' faces seemed haggard, the gargoyles' menacing.

Tyler abruptly backed up and bumped into Avery. "Could he sit any closer to her?" he mumbled.

Avery wondered the same thing. But she couldn't get distracted. "Let's go."

They exited the balcony. Tyler dawdled in front of the second door. "I think this is the tech booth."

"Right," Avery said. They both knew this might be the highest they could get in the building, their last chance to get cell reception.

Tyler cautiously opened the door. Inside, several steps led up to a long room with a window overlooking the stage. In front of the window was a control board featuring dozens of switches, dials, and sliders, even a microphone on a stand. Two office chairs faced a corner, like they'd been put in detention for misbehavior.

Avery immediately checked both phones in her possession. Neither got reception. The hope that she'd been clinging to withered away.

Tyler tapped the control board. "Maybe I can get more lights on."

As he messed with the switches and dials, Avery

zeroed in on a balled-up sandwich wrapper on the floor. She wasn't hungry. Yet. "You didn't bring any food, did you?"

"No. You?" Nothing Tyler did to the board had any effect on the auditorium lighting.

"No. I only have my water bottle. Which is almost empty." Avery gulped. "Paige left hers at the tree house."

"Maybe the water is still on in the building." Tyler flipped a switch.

Avery highly doubted it would be. She gazed helplessly through the window at the stage, vaguely noticing that Jaylen and Paige had risen to their feet. The worries she'd been pushing down inside of her burbled up and poured out. "Tyler, we're in serious trouble."

"Naw." He stayed intent on the controls. Now that he wasn't focused on Jaylen and Paige kissing, his upbeat attitude had returned. "Someone will find us. The owners probably check this place all the time."

"Come on." Avery would've laughed if she weren't so agitated. "Look at this place. No one has been here in months. Maybe years."

Below, Jaylen spun in a slow circle, scanning the stage, still searching. For what, Avery wasn't sure.

Tyler turned a dial. "Once our families figure out that we're gone, they'll come get us."

"How will they even know we're here?" Avery said.

Onstage, Jaylen was saying something to Paige. She shrugged.

"They'll track our phones. Oh, wait. No service." Tyler slid a lever, unbothered. "Well, we'll just have to wait until morning. We can bang on the doors and someone will hear us."

Avery rubbed her eyes. Who was going to come by and hear them? Tyler was so positive he was almost delusional. "Why do you always think things will work out?"

Tyler's focus lingered on the board. "Why don't you?"

"I don't know." Avery adjusted her glasses. As far back as she remembered, she'd always expected the worst thing to happen. "Anxious Avery," her family called her. This past year, it had gotten worse.

Below, Jaylen gestured at the lump the skull made under the drop cloth. Paige cocked her head, then took a hesitant step toward it.

The ghost light blinked once. Then went out.

Immediately, the ghost's glowing figure materialized near the rear wall of the stage, scowling in Paige's direction. Avery gasped.

The light flashed on. The ghost vanished.

"What happened?" Tyler yelped. "I wasn't touching anything, I swear."

"I don't know . . ." The light had only been out a second. Avery wasn't sure what she'd witnessed. Maybe she'd been hallucinating. Yet, while Jaylen still fixated on the drop cloth, Paige gawked at the spot where the ghost had appeared. She'd seen it, too.

The ghost light flickered and dimmed, then grew brighter.

"Oh no," Tyler said. "It's shorting out or something."

Paige wheeled around to face the ghost light. It flickered once more, then everything went black. The ghost reappeared, now on the other side of the drop cloth, closer to Paige. The light sputtered on.

"Paige!" whispered Avery. She pounded on the window. Neither Paige nor Jaylen paid her any attention.

The ghost light began flashing on and off every second like a slow strobe, making all movements on the stage appear jerky. In the dark, Maddie's ghost edged nearer to Paige. In the light, it disappeared while Paige ran to the light stand, and Jaylen—oblivious to the ghost—backed away from the drop cloth.

Tyler grabbed the microphone and lifted it to his mouth. "Jaylen, stop!" The microphone was dead.

"He's going to fall into the grave!" Avery scrambled away from the control board, out the room, and through the balcony door.

"Jaylen!" she yelled.

He glanced toward her just as he took a final step back and tumbled into the hole.

CHAPTER ELEVEN

FROM THE BALCONY, AVERY HEARD JAYLEN HIT THE PLAT-
form at the bottom of the grave with a sickening smack.
The ghost light burst on as the wood snapped beneath
his body and gave way. He plummeted out of sight into
the blackness under the stage.

"Jaylen!" screamed Paige.

Avery spun around and collided with Tyler, who was
racing onto the balcony.

"What happened?" he asked wildly.

"He fell into the basement!" Avery pushed past Tyler
to the stairwell. Images of Jaylen, broken and bloody,
flooded her head. "Come on!"

She and Tyler hurtled down the stairs, their cell lights

flittering around the cement walls. As they entered the lower hall, a frenzied Paige emerged at the other end.

"Hurry, hurry, hurry!" she begged. "We need your lights!"

"Is he okay?" Avery sprinted toward her, Tyler at her heels.

"I don't know!" Paige flattened against the wall and let Avery and her light push ahead into the wings.

Onstage the ghost light was once again steady, no longer strobing, but Avery hardly noticed. The group barreled down the basement stairs.

"What was he doing?" Tyler demanded.

"H-h-he," Paige stuttered. "He was acting bizarre, saying he could hear rats—"

Avery flung open the door to the area under the stage. The putrid stench of death again whacked her in the face. "Jaylen!"

The ghost light streamed through the hole in the stage floor, spotlighting heaps of lighting equipment, ladders, and scenery flats. In the middle of the room, Jaylen was sprawled on his back amid shards of wood and piles of blankets.

"Jaylen!" screeched Paige.

"They're coming!" he yelled.

"Are you hurt?" Avery bulldozed through the junk blocking her path and rushed to his side.

"Get me out of here!" Jaylen pushed up on his elbows.

"Don't move," ordered Tyler. "We have to make sure nothing's broken."

"Don't you see them?" Jaylen pointed into the shadows.

Avery swung her cell light to the corner he indicated and recoiled in disgust. Dozens of squirming rats poured from a hole in the foundation into an opening in the cracked cement floor, their beady eyes glinting red.

"It's okay," she said, trying to reassure herself as much as him. "They're more scared of us than we are of them."

"That's impossible." Jaylen scrabbled halfway to his feet, then yelped and collapsed in a heap. "My ankle!"

His left ankle above his sock had already swelled to twice its normal size.

"Is that all that hurts?" Paige asked.

"Yes!" Jaylen yowled. "Let's go!"

Tyler crouched, nudged his shoulder under Jaylen's left arm, and hoisted him up. Jaylen hopped along on his right foot as fast as he could.

Avery peered up through the hole in the stage. There

was no sign of the ghost. She hurried after the others into the hall, slammed the door behind her, and held her cell up high to light a path.

"It's going to be okay, dude," Tyler said.

"Are the rats coming?" Jaylen sounded desperate.

Avery pictured rats squeezing under the door and swarming after them. She twisted around to check. The hallway behind them was empty. "No."

They floundered up the stairs, Jaylen bracing his right arm against the wall as Tyler boosted his left side. By the time they reached the wings, sweat poured down their faces.

Paige cowered on the top step. "Is the ghost gone?"

"Don't even look," Tyler said. "Let's get him to the dressing room, where that couch is."

They proceeded into the hall and the dressing room. The wig heads watched silently while Tyler eased Jaylen onto the nearest couch. As his weight hit the cushions, a small cloud of dust arose, clogging Avery's lungs and making her cough. Jaylen had gone quiet, his eyes wide and dilated, the black pupils almost obliterating the brown irises.

"I think he's in shock," Paige said. "That's what Brandon looked like when he broke his collarbone."

"We should elevate his foot." Avery heaped pillows under his ankle. Jaylen grimaced.

"He needs something to drink," Tyler said. "I think he brought water. Where's his backpack?"

"On the stage," Paige said. "But I'm not getting it."

Avery scrounged in her backpack for her water. The bottle felt light in her hands. She unscrewed the cap and held the opening to Jaylen's mouth. He lifted his head, swallowed a couple of sips, then sagged onto the pillows.

Tyler turned on the faucets in the sink. There was a groan, a grinding squeal from the pipes in the walls, and an explosive sputter from the spout. A thin trickle of brown water began to run.

"At least they didn't shut the water off," he said.

Paige gagged. "I'm not going to drink that."

"Let it run," Avery suggested. "Maybe it will get better."

Tyler checked his cell phone. "Still no service."

Jaylen moaned.

"Guys." Avery moved closer to the open doorway and waved Tyler and Paige over. She turned her back to Jaylen and lowered her voice. "This is getting serious."

"Getting?" Paige let out a shaky breath.

"What happened on the stage?" Tyler asked her.

"I don't know." Paige tugged nervously on her ponytail. "Jaylen kept saying he could hear rats, but I couldn't at all. Then the light started flashing and the ghost was there and—" Her face crumpled.

Avery drew Paige close in a hug. "The ghost is totally messing with us. Remember, it said it wanted to play? Well, it's playing *tricks.* On us."

"So it made rat sounds?" Tyler said doubtfully. "How is that possible?"

Avery sputtered. Sometimes Tyler was so reasonable, it was ridiculous. "I don't know what ghosts can do! All I know is it's trying to terrorize us."

"Well, it's working," Paige said.

Behind them, Jaylen whimpered.

"What if his ankle is broken?" Avery said.

"I think it is," said Tyler.

"This is an emergency." Paige sniffled, on the verge of tears. "Aren't there, like, emergency exits in places like this?"

"There are, but everything's locked," Tyler said.

"Wait!" Avery exclaimed. "What about one of those fire alarms with a lever that you pull down? Maybe we can set one off!"

"Brilliant," Tyler said.

Hope dawned across Paige's face. "Then the fire

department will come rescue us. And bring an ambulance for sure."

Avery played her light across the dressing room walls. "There's no alarm in here, though."

"Maybe there is one by the back door." Tyler poked his head into the hall and aimed his cell light to the end. As Avery and Paige peered over his shoulder, the light illuminated a small red box protruding from the wall, about five feet above the floor.

"Yes!" Paige said.

"I'm going to try it," Tyler said. "Stay here with Jaylen."

Avery and Paige hovered in the doorway, watching, while he ventured down the hall. The closer he got to the wings, the faster Avery's heart beat. What if Maddie's ghost was lying in wait, about to strike? "Be careful!" she hissed.

But Tyler passed the stage door with no attack from the ghost. At the alarm, he positioned his hand on the lever and glanced their way. "Ready? One, two, three!" He pulled it.

Avery cringed, bracing for a piercing wail. But nothing happened. Tyler uselessly shoved the lever up and down several times.

Paige sank into Avery's side. "Oh no."

For a split second, Tyler's shoulders slumped in defeat. Then he straightened and trotted back to the dressing room. "Okay, we can't hear it, but it could still be signaling the fire station." He acted upbeat, but his voice wavered.

Paige nodded vigorously. "Right? They're probably on their way."

Avery gnawed her thumbnail. "How long will it take?"

"Five minutes? Or less? I mean, there's no traffic." Tyler attempted a smile.

"Let's listen for the sirens," Paige said.

Tyler settled on a chair near the makeup counter and jiggled his leg. Paige paced. Avery concentrated as hard as she could for the slightest hint of a far-off siren. Instead, the silence roared, louder than ever, broken every minute or so by Jaylen taking a hissed breath. He had fallen into a restless slumber on the couch, often shifting position and grimacing in pain.

They waited. Time crawled.

After about five minutes, Avery cleared her throat. "Nobody's coming, you guys."

"There must be more fire alarms," Tyler said. "We should try all of them."

"We can't leave Jaylen alone, though," Avery pointed out.

"I'm glad he's asleep," Paige said. "He's exhausted. Avery, will you stay with him? I'll go with Tyler and find the other fire alarms."

"Awesome!" Tyler leapt to his feet, clearly flattered he'd been chosen, then faltered. He awkwardly flipped his hair. "That works," he added casually.

"I gotta do something, instead of just waiting," Paige said, wringing her hands. "It hurts to see Jaylen hurt. You know?"

Tyler wilted, but played it cool. "Totally. That good with you, Aves?"

"I guess," Avery said doubtfully.

"You got this, Aves," Paige said. "Someone has to stay with Jaylen, and Tyler can't go alone."

Afraid as she was, Avery couldn't argue with that logic. "Okay. But please be careful."

She walked them to the door, not wanting to let them out of her sight.

"Let's try the lobby first," Tyler said.

He and Paige drifted down the hall, their voices growing softer. Avery watched until the darkness swallowed them whole.

CHAPTER TWELVE

AFTER PAIGE AND TYLER FADED AWAY, AVERY RETURNED TO the dressing room. Jaylen's eyes were closed. If he wasn't awake, she might as well be alone. A horrible thought occurred to her. What if . . .

She sped to his side. The rational part of her brain told her she was overreacting, but she still leaned over him, checking to make sure he was breathing. For one awful moment she couldn't tell if he was, then she spotted a slight rise and fall of his chest. Okay, he wasn't dead. Thank goodness.

Avery restlessly settled on the other couch. The room was sweltering. She ripped off her hoodie and stuffed it into her backpack.

The time on her phone read two forty-five, which seemed impossibly early. Maybe the clock wasn't working right, either. So much had happened since her plane landed twelve hours ago, it felt like days had passed. Not only had she discovered countless ways her friends had changed, but she herself—scaredy-cat Avery, of all people—had suggested a séance. They'd snuck into an abandoned theater late at night. They'd seen a terrifying ghost. And now they were trapped with that ghost, a ghost that at best wanted to mess with them and at worst wanted to do them harm. Whether it could control rats or imitate their sounds, Avery had no clue. But she knew the ghost was somehow responsible for Jaylen's fall. A fall that could have killed him.

Avery examined Jaylen's sleeping face, which had grown up so much since she'd moved away. He might be even more handsome than Russell. The thought made her smile. Jaylen would be thrilled to best his brother in any way. Paige had probably noticed Jaylen's appearance changing, too. Maybe that was why she kissed him.

Avery's smile faded as the reality of that kiss sank in again. To her, Jaylen would always be the talkative buddy she'd walked to preschool with, the sweet friend who'd helped her pull out her first loose tooth when she'd thought she couldn't take the pain, the enthusiastic teacher who'd coached her to jump off the high dive at age nine, even though she'd been terrified. As tough as he'd been acting today, Jaylen's heart was unbelievably kind. They had to get him out of this place and to a hospital.

A thump came from the ceiling above her. Every muscle in Avery's body tensed, until she heard another thump and another. Okay, it was only Tyler and Paige's footsteps as they checked the second floor for fire alarms.

Her gaze landed on the foam heads lining the makeup counter. There was quite a variety of hair represented— a long, red, wavy mane; a short, boyish blond one; a dark, cropped, curly one. Behind the heads, the mirror reflected a costume rack near the door. What if Maddie's ghost lurked amid the voluminous gowns, spying on her, waiting for the chance to pounce?

Avery pushed off the couch, frustrated. She needed to keep her mind occupied or her imagination would spiral out of control. She spotted a play program on the makeup counter. Perfect. She picked it up.

The cover was identical to the *Hamlet* poster from the lobby. Even in smaller form, the skull gave Avery the creeps. She hastily flipped to the first page.

The program began with an open letter from the leader of the Midnight Players. It detailed their mission—how they hoped their productions would bring culture, entertainment, and joy to the community. Avery felt a pang of sadness. The players never would've guessed how their theater company would come to an end.

She skipped the note about the playhouse's renovation and focused on the photos of its grand reopening. The auditorium, with the frescoes vibrantly painted and the cupid sculptures intact, was dazzling and welcoming, not at all like the depressing space only a hall away from her. One photo featured a beaming woman onstage wearing a colorful fringed scarf draped dramatically around her neck. The caption identified her as the theater season's director, Maddie's mom. In the background, a curly-haired blond girl peeked around the side curtain. *Maddie,* Avery thought. She brought the program closer to her face and studied it. Maddie definitely had a mischievous glint in her eyes. But not mischievous in any evil way, more like playful. She appeared poised to scamper across the stage and surprise her mom. Avery's heart sank and she quickly turned the page.

The next section was about *Hamlet* and its history. Avery skimmed through until she caught a mention of the "graveyard" scene and then read with interest. Apparently, it was the most famous scene in the play, the part where Hamlet the prince says the famous words "To be or not to be, that is the question." She vaguely remembered her mom telling her that the point of the scene was that everyone dies. No matter how rich or poor anyone is in life, everyone ends up in the same place— the grave.

Avery shuddered. She didn't need to think about death right now.

She reached the last pages of the program, where the entire team was credited. Scanning through the short paragraphs, her attention landed on the props master, Alexandria Jones. Her bio described how eager she was to explore the Midwest as a lifelong New Englander. She enjoyed finding props at estate sales, in old attics and garages, and in specialty shops. Her favorite discovery was a cauldron from Massachusetts that she planned to use someday in the witches' scene from Shakespeare's *Macbeth*. Avery wondered where Alexandria had found the skull.

She scrutinized the small photo next to the bio. The props master was an older woman, dressed in a cloak-like black dress and shawl. Her eyes were oddly intense.

Unnerved, Avery closed the program and dropped it on the counter.

A low laugh erupted behind her. She twisted around.

Jaylen lay on his side, his elbow bent, head propped on his hand, glaring at her.

"Oh!" Avery clamped her hand to her chest, startled. "How's your ankle?"

His mouth stretched into that same, awful jack-o-lantern grin from the séance, although there was no candle under his chin.

"Avery," he whispered, unblinking. "The rats are all around us."

"What?" She jumped from the stool, raising her arms out from her sides, palms spread, ready for combat. "Where?"

"They were on the stage," Jaylen said. "Under that cloth you put over the skull."

Avery straightened out of her useless pose. "They were?"

"I saw the cloth wiggling. And heard the rats squealing."

He winked at her.

Avery gave him the side-eye. "You did?" Something was not right with him.

"Yes. The rats are everywhere." Jaylen rapped sharply on the wood-paneled wall next to him. "In fact, they're hiding in here right now." He slid his right foot onto the floor as if he wanted to stand.

"Don't get up." Avery darted over to him and placed her hands on his shoulders. His body temperature was surprisingly cold through his T-shirt. Was that another symptom of shock? His creepy grin stayed in place.

"Okay, Jaylen." She used the soothing voice she put on whenever Julia had a nightmare and needed to go back to sleep. "You should lie down and get some rest. We're going to get you out of here."

He allowed her to press him back against the pillows but raised an eyebrow. "Really." The word wasn't a question.

"Yes." Avery grabbed a frayed, crocheted throw from the other couch and draped it over him. "Tyler and Paige went to find all the fire alarms and pull them. Then help will come."

Jaylen's laugh was so quick and harsh Avery almost wondered if she'd imagined it. "Good luck with that," he said. "We'll be rat food before anyone ever finds us."

Avery reared back. "Jaylen!"

"You know it's the truth." He pulled one of his braids. "We won't last for more than a few days without food or water."

"Nope. No." Avery gritted her teeth. He was saying out loud the fears she'd been fighting to smother. She would not listen. "That's not going to happen."

"The rats will get us," he continued, "and only bones will be left by the time they find us. We'll be exactly like the skull."

"Stop it," Avery snapped. She slammed shut the corner of her mind that argued he might be right. Nope. Jaylen was obviously delirious with pain and talking nonsense. She channeled Tyler again. In the tech booth, he'd been convinced they'd be rescued. "In the morning, someone will come by and we'll yell—"

"You don't believe that," Jaylen said.

Avery stiffened. Was she that transparent? "Sure, I do."

He sighed and stuck out his lower lip like a toddler. "I wish I could go back onstage."

"Why? Would you feel better near the ghost light?" Avery asked. On one hand, when the ghost light was functioning right, it kept the ghost away, so the stage wasn't a bad place to be. On the other, the light wasn't exactly reliable, and the ghost hadn't found them in the dressing room. It could be best to stay hidden offstage.

"No." Jaylen laid back, his hands behind his head. "I want to play."

"Play what?" Avery said hesitantly, reminded of the ghost's awful invitation on the phone. "The piano?"

"That's for me to know and you to find out." His voice was a childish singsong. Goose bumps broke out all over Avery's skin.

She rubbed her arms to stop the tingling and rolled her eyes. "Okay, sure." If she focused on how annoying he was being, she wouldn't be scared.

"Actually, you should go play, Avery." Jaylen's mouth settled again into that joyless smile. "Go have fun onstage."

Avery forced herself to casually flop onto the other couch. "Yeah, no, I'm gonna stay here with you."

"Suit yourself." Jaylen began to hum a tune. It sounded familiar to Avery, but he was so off-key, she couldn't pick up what it was. She watched the door. Where the heck were Paige and Tyler?

They sat without speaking for a few minutes. Then Jaylen's humming ceased. He'd fallen asleep again. His eyes moved frantically behind his closed eyelids, back and forth, back and forth.

The movement reminded Avery of something. Something that had recently happened. But what?

She caught her breath.

It reminded her of Maddie pacing on the balcony.

Panic filled her. What if . . . what if Maddie's ghost had somehow possessed Jaylen? The ghost could be pranking them by disguising itself as one of them. Jaylen was acting completely unlike himself. They'd already witnessed a ghost in real life. Was the idea of possession so far-fetched?

She needed Tyler and Paige. Why weren't they back yet?

Avery rose and tiptoed to the doorway. The hall was deserted, but the glow from the ghost light spilled from the wings onto the floor. A slight sound drifted through the air. She tilted her head and listened. It was the tinkling of piano music. The name of the tune popped into her head: "Rock-a-Bye Baby." Avery flashed back to their hike through Crawley Woods, from what seemed like days ago. That had been the song that Duke Olsen's cousin claimed to hear coming from the theater.

Now that she thought about it, that was the same song Jaylen had hummed moments ago.

Avery's skin crawled. "Paige?" she called shakily. "Tyler?"

No one answered. The piano music continued.

A burning curiosity ignited inside her. Who was in the auditorium? She took one step forward, inexplicably drawn to the stage. Her rational mind told her not to go anywhere. But Jaylen was okay; he was asleep. She'd only be gone a second.

Avery crept along the hall. "Paige?"

A shadow crossed the light spread across the hall floor in front of her. Someone had passed in front of the ghost light onstage.

"Is that you guys?"

The piano music abruptly cut off. A new sound began, a low rumble. Avery couldn't understand what it could possibly be.

The séance candle that she'd lost onstage slowly rolled from the wings into the hall and halted. Avery froze. Where had it come from? She held her breath, waiting for its next move.

The candle leisurely retreated into the wings and

out of sight. Avery had a desperate urge to chase it. She stepped forward, drawn to the stage.

Something banged behind her. Avery whipped around as Tyler and Paige emerged from the stairwell.

"What are you doing, Aves?" Tyler asked.

"I . . . I . . ." Avery shook her head, fighting to clear her sudden confusion. "I don't know . . . I thought . . ."

Paige moved to her and grasped her arm. "Are you okay? Is Jaylen?"

Avery started to tremble. That was right, she'd heard music coming from the auditorium. But Paige and Tyler had come from the other direction. Neither of them could've been at the piano only seconds before. She put her hand on the wall to steady herself. "Did you guys hear that?"

Tyler stared at her. "Hear what?"

"Never mind." Avery tried to get a hold of herself. Now the ghost was playing tricks on *her*. Or was she imagining it? Maybe she was hearing things, like Jaylen. "I'm fine. Did you guys find anything?"

Tyler exhaled dejectedly. "We found a couple more fire alarms, one in the lobby and one upstairs. We pulled them, but nothing happened."

"How's Jaylen?" Paige asked.

"He's asleep." Avery hesitated. "He's saying weird stuff."

"Like what?" Tyler asked.

"Um, well, he basically said we were going to end up rat food. He's kind of freaking me out, actually." Avery stopped herself from sharing her suspicions. Jaylen might be possessed, but she didn't have enough proof to say that for a fact. She had to learn more before she discussed it at all. The last thing they needed right now was more arguing.

"I told you, he's in shock," Paige said.

Tyler stilled. "I wonder if he got a concussion when he fell."

Avery hadn't thought of that. "Oh no. Then he probably shouldn't be asleep, right?"

All three of them rushed to Jaylen and woke him up. He blinked at them, his gaze focused but distant. Paige held his hand, begging him not to drift off.

"Fine, fine," Jaylen said grumpily.

Tyler flopped down on the opposite couch. "Okay, let's try to get some rest," he said. "Everything will look better in the morning."

"Sleep?" Avery huffed. "How can I sleep?"

"Just lie down, then," Tyler said. "No sense in

exhausting ourselves. There's nothing we can do until morning. Someone will come by. I know it."

"Is it safe to go to sleep?" Paige eyed Jaylen apprehensively. "One of us should stay up with him, right?"

"I'll keep watch and make sure he stays awake," Tyler said. "We'll take turns. You guys sleep for now and I'll wake one of you up in an hour or something."

Avery relaxed the tiniest bit. Even if Tyler was faking his composure, it helped to know someone was taking the lead.

There was no way she'd sleep, though.

CHAPTER THIRTEEN

SOMEWHERE, SOMEONE LAUGHED, A HIGH-PITCHED CAC-
kle. Avery's eyes snapped open. She peered around the
dimly lit room, confused. Where was she?

Paige snored lightly next to her on the same lumpy
couch, but this wasn't the Sernetts' basement. Someone
else leaned forward on a chair—oh, it was Tyler—his
head of shaggy hair rested atop his folded arms on a desk
of some kind. A cell phone near his elbow shone its light
straight up at a water-stained ceiling.

Avery shot upright, a stream of images flooding
her brain: The paneless basement window framing black
space. The open-mouthed ghost falling at her. The skull
peering around the tombstone.

Worst of them all: Jaylen flat on his back under the open hole in the stage.

Oh no. Tyler had fallen asleep. What about Jaylen? Avery whipped around to face the other couch.

Jaylen lay there peacefully, eyes fixed on the ceiling, his fingers tapping on his legs like he was drumming to music in his head. He seemed fine. She should let Tyler sleep and be the person on watch for now. Avery checked around the room to make sure everything else was okay. Her breath hitched.

Beyond Tyler's elbow, nestled among the blank-faced wig heads, lurked the skull.

Avery screamed.

"What?" Paige jerked, limbs flailing.

Tyler jolted awake. "I'm up!"

Avery pointed a shaking finger at the skull. "Look!"

"What the—" Tyler scooted backward in the chair, its feet screeching across the floor.

Paige shrieked. "How'd that get in here?"

"I don't know!" Tyler rubbed his eyes. "I must've fallen asleep. I'm sorry!"

The same high-pitched cackle that had awakened Avery burst from Jaylen's mouth. She turned on him. "Did you bring that skull in here?"

Jaylen swept his hands toward his elevated foot. "Uh, no. I can hardly walk."

A terrible mixture of rage and anxiety churned inside Avery. Had Maddie's ghost truly possessed him? "Then what's so funny?"

Jaylen shrugged. "This whole situation."

The skull watched, its lipless mouth grinning on, like it was pleased with their bickering.

"Do something, Tyler!" Paige yelped.

Tyler sprang forward, reaching for the skull.

All of a sudden, a howling wind blew in from the hallway, slamming the door to the wall, pinning Avery and Paige to the couch and almost knocking Tyler flat. But he pushed ahead, regaining his balance, and seized the skull. He spun right, then left, like he didn't know what to do, then broke for the lockers. Battling the wind, he wrestled open the nearest locker, hurled the skull inside, and closed the door. The wind abruptly ceased.

Jaylen snorted with amusement.

"What is happening?" Tyler asked, his hair blown every which way.

"Did the ghost move the skull?" Paige whispered.

"I told you guys." Avery's voice quavered. "It's playing games with us. It said it wanted to, and it is."

"But I don't want to play games," Paige whimpered.

"This room is too small." Tyler began to pace. "I don't feel safe in here anymore."

"Nowhere is safe," said Jaylen ominously.

"Cut it out," Avery said to him. "You're not helping." *Whoever you are.* She glared at him. He smirked back.

"I don't want to stay here with the skull," Paige said.

Avery pictured it inside the locker, spying on them through the vents in the metal.

Tyler pulled his T-shirt away from his neck. "It's hard to breathe in here."

Avery felt for him. He'd always had trouble in small spaces.

"Let's go back to the auditorium," Paige said. "The ghost light is in there. I mean, at least the ghost stays away when it's on."

Avery twisted her bracelet. "But what if it starts strobing again?"

"Do you have a better idea?" Tyler snapped.

Avery blinked, startled. Tyler never talked like that. His face was pinched and he was breathing hard. "What about Jaylen, though?"

"I'll go," Jaylen said almost cheerfully. "It doesn't matter where we are, anyway. The rats will get us eventually."

"Please," Paige begged. "Stop it."

"I gotta get out of here," Tyler said frantically. "Jaylen, try to stand."

"Yes, sir." Jaylen hopped up on his good foot and slung his arm over Tyler's shoulder. Together they staggered toward the doorway.

"Fine. Let's go." Avery snatched her backpack. No sense letting Tyler's claustrophobia overwhelm him. Plus, she didn't feel safe in the dressing room anymore, either. Not with the skull there.

In the hallway, Tyler grunted in frustration. "Can't you move any faster?" His shirt, drenched with sweat, clung to his back.

"What do you think?" Jaylen sneered.

Paige hustled to Jaylen's side opposite Tyler and scooped her shoulder under his free arm. "Here, hold on to our hands, Jay. Tyler, put your other hand behind his knee."

Tyler did, and together they lifted Jaylen's legs, making a chair for him. They all moved to the wings and onto the stage. Avery scooped up Jaylen's backpack as she passed it. The ghost light shone steadily, and there was no sign of the ghost.

Stepping down the risers to the seats, she scrutinized

the piano in the orchestra pit. As far as she could tell, the thick layer of dust on its keys remained undisturbed by any fingerprints. Avery imagined unseen fingers pressing the piano keys, a haunting version of "Rock-a-Bye Baby" hypnotizing them all, and the ghost coming for them.

She forced the thought away.

After some debate, they decided to position Jaylen in the front row. If he slouched low enough, he could elevate his ankle on top of the short wall that separated the audience from the orchestra pit yet remain in the protective glow of the ghost light. Tyler and Paige sat next to him.

Avery ditched the backpacks in an empty seat in the second row. She checked Jaylen's for a water bottle but found nothing.

"Maybe ghosts go away when the sun rises," Paige said hopefully.

Jaylen laughed his new harsh laugh, a sound more mocking than amused.

"What?" Paige said. "You should hope they do."

Tyler covered his face with his hands. "We're doomed, you know," he said through his fingers. "The walls are closing in."

"Okay, Tyler." Avery assumed he was joking, until he lowered his hands and she caught his grim expression. They'd left the dressing room. Why hadn't his claustrophobic feelings gone away?

"At least we're in in a big area." He nodded. "It will take a while."

"Take a while for . . . ?" Avery waited.

Tyler sighed as if she was brainless. "For the walls to move in and crush us."

Paige straightened in her seat. "What are you talking about?"

"You don't believe me? Come here." Tyler swiftly stood and crossed in front of her.

"No thanks," Paige said, shrinking away from him.

Tyler sidled along a row of seats until it ended at the wall. After a moment of uncertainty, Avery got up and tagged behind him. He placed his palm over one of the terrified horses. "There. Do you feel it?"

Avery gingerly touched the plaster. The surface was disgustingly slick, as if it was sweating along with Tyler. But it was solid and still. "Tyler," she said as steadily as she could. "The walls aren't moving."

"Oh yes, they are," he leaned close to her, his eyes bleak. "You'll see. We're doomed."

Avery backed away from him, a terrible certainty growing inside her. This wasn't Tyler talking. The ghost had possessed him, like it had Jaylen. How long until it infected Paige's mind? And then her own? Would she even know if she was possessed? Did Tyler or Jaylen have any idea? Their true selves could be struggling inside their bodies, losing the war to expel the ghost. She stumbled into the aisle.

"What is his deal?" Paige asked Avery under her breath.

Avery thought fast. Her best friend was still herself, at least for the moment. They had to talk away from the guys and to figure out a game plan before anything else awful happened.

"I need to use the bathroom," Avery blurted so loudly that Paige startled in her seat. "Paige, when you guys were searching for the fire alarms, did you find any other restrooms?"

"Uh, yeah." Paige frowned. "In the lobby."

"Great, will you go with me, please? I don't want to go alone."

"Girls, always going to the bathroom together . . . ," Jaylen quipped.

Avery ignored him, instead directing all the psychic

energy she had at Paige, staring her down. *If you were ever my BFF, please go with this.*

"Okay." Paige nodded, miraculously understanding. "Right. And let's check if the water works there."

"You two take care now, okay?" Jaylen winked.

"Stick together," Tyler added. He ran his hands along the wall despondently.

"Right," Avery said. She had to act natural. Who knew what would happen if Jaylen or Tyler—or the ghost, really—realized she was onto them.

Avery and Paige trudged up the aisle toward the lobby. Before they exited the auditorium, Avery peered back at the guys.

Both stared straight at her, watching her.

CHAPTER FOURTEEN

WHEN THEY ENTERED THE LOBBY, PAIGE POINTED WORD-
lessly to two doors past the coat check. Avery automatically bypassed the one labeled "men's" before it registered how ridiculous it was to obey any rules in this desperate situation.

The ladies' room smelled rank and stale. Thick humidity dampened Avery's skin. She dragged a tall metal trash can to the threshold to prop open the door and then faced Paige.

"Do you really have to use the bathroom?" Paige wrinkled her nose.

"No," Avery said. "We just need to talk."

"Seriously?" Paige swiped a flyaway lock of hair off her face. "We could've talked in the theater."

"I didn't want the guys to hear."

"Why not?"

"Uh . . ." Avery had no clue how to start the conversation.

Paige slapped open one of the stall doors. "Well, now I actually have to go. Power of suggestion, I guess." She shut herself inside.

A soft thud came from the lobby. Avery flinched and listened for more. But all she could hear was Paige doing her business. She caught a glimpse of a haunted face in the mirror above the sinks and her throat tightened. But it was only her own reflection, with bruise-like shadows etched under her eyes. She looked like a character in one of the horror movies she hated. If only this was a movie and not her real life.

She shouldn't waste another second. The ghost could possess her or Paige at any time. "Okay, something weird is going on with the guys," Avery started.

"I know." Paige's voice ricocheted around the tiled walls. "When even Tyler gives up hope, things are bad. I don't know how much more of this I can take."

"I think it's worse than that," Avery said. "They're . . . not themselves." Every stall door was closed. She imagined one flying open and the ghost lunging at her, the horrible mouth opening wide, ready to swallow her whole.

"Huh?"

Avery scrambled to figure how she could possibly explain her theory to Paige. "I think . . . somehow Maddie has gotten into their heads."

The stall door creaked open, and Paige emerged. "Mine, too," she said bitterly.

Avery went rigid. "What do you mean?"

"What do you think I mean? I'm terrified." Paige strode to the sink and turned on the faucet. No water came out. She gripped the counter and bowed her head. "Of course there's no water. What was I thinking?" Her voice was tinged with hysteria.

Avery twisted her hands together. "No, I mean, it's literally like the ghost is *in* their heads. Possessing them."

"Come on, Aves." Paige cast her a panicked look in the mirror. "You can't lose it, too."

"I'm not, I swear. Jaylen is acting totally bizarre, not like himself at all. And Ty—"

"Ghosts are one thing. Possession is another." Paige nodded, like that was a perfectly reasonable thing to say.

"That makes no sense."

"I'm not going to listen to this."

"But—"

"I can't, I can't, I can't!" Paige shook her head violently, making her ponytail fly. "Just stop, okay? I don't want to talk about this!"

"We have to." Avery tried to place a grounding hand on Paige's shoulder, but Paige skittered away from her.

"I wish this was all a bad dream!" Paige screwed her eyes shut.

"So do I!" Avery said. "But it's not. What should we do?"

"How would I know?" Paige wheeled around and stuck her index finger in Avery's face. "You need to fix this. This is all your fault."

Avery's mouth fell open. "What?"

"This whole thing was *your* idea." Paige planted her hands on her hips.

"But . . ." The guilt Avery had been battling for hours in the back of her mind exploded like a bomb. It *was* her fault.

Paige's face reddened. "You're even the reason we're stuck in here. The stupid chair you picked wasn't heavy enough to hold the door. So now we're trapped."

"Whoa!" Avery's hackles rose. True, she'd chosen the wrong chair, but it wasn't like she'd done that on purpose. Paige had gone too far. "I never wanted to come in here. Jaylen was the one who climbed through a broken window and told everyone else to come inside. And you and Tyler jumped right in."

"Who cares?" Paige scoffed. "We wouldn't even have been here if it wasn't for you!"

"That's not fair!" Anger surged through Avery's veins. "I thought you'd say no from the beginning. You've always been scared to death of ghosts. I never *ever* thought you'd go along with this séance stuff!"

"Oh, so you were counting on me to stop this?" Paige narrowed her eyes. "Way to take responsibility."

Again, Paige was right, but Avery refused to admit it. She pivoted from defense to offense. "Why are you so mad at me? I should be mad at *you*! You're the one who has totally changed. It's like you're a completely different person."

Paige tsked. "I am not."

"Yes, you are! Wearing makeup and shopping and

hanging out with Bethany Barnes." Avery spit out the name.

"So what?" Paige clenched her fists. "Bethany is my friend. I can tell her things—"

"Like how you kissed Jaylen?"

Paige's defiant attitude wavered. Then she raised her chin stubbornly. "Yes! Exactly!"

Avery shrank back, bumping into a stall door. Her worst fear was confirmed. This was the ultimate betrayal. "You told Bethany and you didn't tell me?"

"Well, she actually listens." Paige's clenched fists went slack at her sides.

Tears stung Avery's eyes. "But I thought I was your best friend."

"I thought you were, too," Paige said. "But things change, Avery. Whether you want them to or not. And you have to deal with that."

"What are you talking about?"

Paige threw up her hands. "Avery, you live in Philly now. That's the way it is. Accept it."

Avery's anger flared. Paige had no idea what the past year had been like for her. "You try moving away from everyone and everything you've ever known."

Paige's face softened. "I'm sure it's been hard. I *know*

it has. And I was right there with you at first. But you never even tried to fit in at your new school."

Avery bristled. "I did so."

"No, you didn't. You didn't join clubs or swim team or anything like you did here."

"They don't have swim team!" Avery shot back.

"Then try something else! Aves, all you've talked about for the last year is how miserable you've been. You called me every day for months and months to complain about school and your parents. And after a while—"

"After a while, what? You decided you didn't like me anymore? Because I was sad?" Avery was outraged. How could someone be so cruel?

"No!" Paige slapped her hand on the sink in frustration. "Because it was always all about you! I tried to talk to you, but you never listened to *me*. Just like you aren't listening now!"

"What are you talking about?"

Paige took a deep breath. "Do you know how lucky you are?" she continued quietly. "Your parents are amazing."

"Yeah, so amazing that they ripped me away from my home," Avery grumbled. She still couldn't forgive her parents.

"Well, at least they have time for you. Natalie and

Brandon and I have practically been taking care of ourselves. All my parents do is argue with each other. They're getting a divorce."

"They are?" Avery was stunned. The Sernetts had always been the most perfect family on the block. "Why didn't you tell me?"

Paige groaned. "I tried. This is my point. I even tried to tell you about Jaylen, but you kept on talking about yourself. Bethany actually *listens* to me."

Avery's stomach lurched. Everything Paige was saying rang true, as much as she wished it didn't. She'd been so wrapped up in her own problems she didn't even listen to her best friend. Her anger from moments before melted into heavy, unshakable guilt.

A giggle came from the lobby.

Avery's eyes met Paige's in the mirror. "Did you hear that?"

"Tyler?" Paige called weakly.

They waited, straining their ears for the slightest sound. None came.

"What if it's the ghost?" The color drained from Paige's cheeks. "Should we hide?"

"Let's get back to the ghost light," Avery whispered.

Paige nodded. Avery led the way, Paige clutching the

bottom hem of her T-shirt from behind like a lifeline. They tiptoed out of the bathroom, sweeping their cell lights around the lobby. Everything appeared the same. The auditorium door was only a few yards away. As they snuck toward it, all the hairs on the back of Avery's neck lifted. Her instincts screamed at her. Something was terribly wrong.

Then she saw it.

The skull.

CHAPTER FIFTEEN

THE SKULL RESTED ON THE GLASS DISPLAY CASE BETWEEN
the girls and the auditorium door, as if an unseen hand
had picked it up and placed it there.

Paige gave a strangled cry. "Go away!" She surged
forward, reaching toward the skull.

"No!" Avery was struck by a horrible revelation. She
launched her body between Paige and the skull, stopping
her inches from the display case.

Paige, frantic and frenzied, tried to push past her.
"We have to get rid of it!"

"Don't touch it!" Avery gripped Paige's hands. "That's
how it happens!"

Paige struggled, but Avery held fast. "How what happens?"

"How Maddie gets in your head!"

"Not this again!" Paige wailed.

"Think about it!" Avery said. "Right after Jaylen picked up the skull onstage, he started hearing rats everywhere. He's terrified of rats. And after Tyler touched it in the dressing room, he freaked about the walls closing in. He's claustrophobic!"

Paige gaped at her. "So?"

"The skull is the connection! I don't know how, but the ghost must use the skull to get into someone's mind and find out their biggest fear. Then it uses that to torture them!"

"But—"

"Please, Paige," Avery begged. "Even if you don't believe me, don't take a chance. *Please.*"

"Fine." Paige jerked her hands out of Avery's and stepped back. "But we have to do something!"

Avery knew she was right. They needed to stop Maddie's sick game. But how? The skull sat there, silent, sullen, seemingly self-satisfied. Avery's frustration boiled over.

She latched on to the nearby broom by its bristles,

lifted it, and brought it down hard on the top of the skull. But the broom's metal handle bounced off the bone without causing the slightest dent. Avery walloped it again and got the same result. In desperation she hoisted the handle high over her head and smashed it down with all her might. The blow forced the skull to spurt to one side, and the broom continued downward, hammering the counter with full force. Waves of pain radiated up Avery's arms. The glass shattered with an earsplitting crack, and shards of glass flew, slicing the air.

Avery chucked the broom to the floor. Paige threw her hands up to shield her face, her cell light arcing up to the ceiling, and took off blindly in the direction of the auditorium door. She tripped, arms pinwheeling, and fell hard on her side.

She screamed.

"Paige!" Avery raced to her.

Paige aimed her light at her thigh. A jagged glass shard jutted from her skin. Screaming again, she plucked it out and hurled it across the lobby. Blood gushed from the wound. Her face went blank. "Oh no."

"Hold on!" Avery desperately tried to recall the first aid lessons from the babysitting class she'd taken at the Y.

Pressure. Tourniquet.

She shrugged her backpack from her shoulders and snatched her hoodie.

"I—I—I . . . ," Paige stuttered.

"Shhhh." Avery cinched the sleeves around Paige's leg above the cut, then bunched up the rest of the hoodie and pressed it into the skin to staunch the blood. "Tyler! Help!" she yelled, hoping against hope he'd listen and come to his senses. She couldn't do this alone.

Paige's face paled and her eyelids fluttered. Avery caught her head before it hit the ground. "Stay with me! Help me get you to the ghost light!"

Paige took a shuddering breath and rallied. Avery shouldered her backpack, hitched her arms under Paige's, and together they lurched to their feet. She shot a glance at the skull. It sat unmoving amid the remains of the glass counter on the case's middle shelf. Their sneakers crunched on broken glass as they hobbled to the auditorium door. Avery yanked it open and dragged Paige across the threshold.

Tyler and Jaylen faced the stage, only the backs of their heads visible above the top of the seats. The ghost light flickered ominously.

"Tyler! Help me!" Avery yelled.

He didn't budge. Neither did Jaylen. Avery maneuvered a weakening Paige down the aisle as fast as she could.

How much blood loss was too much?

At the second row, Paige's legs buckled, and Avery eased her into a seat across the aisle from the guys. She racked her brain, thinking back to something about blood flow and circulation.

"We need to get your leg up to slow the bleeding," she said, helping Paige drape her injured leg over the seat in front of her. But that positioned the blood-soaked tourniquet level with Paige's face. Paige took one look and her eyes rolled back into her head. She passed out.

"Guys!" Avery said helplessly. "She's really hurt. What are we going to do?"

Tyler finally acknowledged her presence. "There's nothing to do but wait."

"Wait for what?" Avery's voice cracked.

"Wait for the walls to pulverize us," Tyler said, rocking back and forth.

"Wait for the rats to get us," Jaylen said, pulling one of his braids so hard Avery thought he'd rip it from his scalp.

Something inside her broke. This was no game. The

ghost was just a kid. How could it be so vicious? Avery charged at Tyler, seized his shoulders, and shook him. "Snap out of it, Ty!" His mop of hair flopped into his eyes. He didn't answer.

Jaylen giggled.

These were not her friends. Avery released Tyler and backed into the wall in front of the orchestra pit. "Maddie, why are you doing this?" she called despairingly.

Jaylen and Tyler gloated at her. Avery spun around and addressed the catwalk. "Maddie, I'm sorry that we disturbed you! We should have let you rest. But please, stop torturing us! I need my friends back!"

There was no response.

Avery slid down the dividing wall until she bumped onto the floor. A few hours ago, she'd been in danger of losing her closest friendships. For a brief time, she'd won them back. But now their actual lives were threatened. She could lose her friends for real.

It was over. They were doomed.

Even if they weren't possessed, the guys were useless. Jaylen couldn't walk and was convinced rats were after them. Tyler had given up hope and was hallucinating that the walls were closing in. Paige was unconscious and possibly bleeding to death. Even if she survived the blood loss, she couldn't live more than a few days without water. None of them could.

Only Avery could rescue them. But there was no way out of the building, no way to call for help. She was only thirteen. How was she supposed to save them all?

Avery gave in and let her worries spiral out of control. She wondered what their families would think happened to them. Her parents might believe she'd run away. She hadn't been shy about telling them that moving for their "stupid" teaching jobs had ruined her life. She covered her face with her hands. How could she have been so hateful? Then there was Julia. Avery hadn't been exactly nice to her the last few months, jealous that her little sister made friends much more easily than she did. Julia would grow up without her big sister, probably hating her.

Avery imagined the frantic calls between their parents later that day. Maybe the families would think the kids had been kidnapped by someone who'd escaped the local jail. They'd wait for a ransom call that never came. Meanwhile, their children would starve to death only a mile from Ridge Road, praying they'd be rescued by people who couldn't find them.

At some point, the sheriff might drag Clear Creek for their bodies. The whole town would come out to observe on the first day, but the crowd would dwindle over time when nothing surfaced. Gradually the citizens would resume their normal lives. Avery, Paige, Jaylen, and Tyler would become a distant memory, a cautionary tale used to get other kids in town to behave.

Eventually, they'd all be forgotten.

Avery lowered her head to her knees and let her tears flow. If only she'd tried harder in Philadelphia. If she'd made new friends, she wouldn't have been so anxious to impress her old friends. She never would've suggested going to an abandoned theater and having a séance. She would've had more confidence. She would've believed in herself.

Avery choked back a sob. The boys stirred.

"Hush now," Tyler said soothingly.

"Don't worry," Jaylen added. "It's not so bad."

Avery raised her head. To her surprise, Tyler had stopped rocking and Jaylen no longer tugged his braids. Instead they regarded her kindly.

"Isn't this what you want, Avery? For nothing to change?" Tyler asked.

"Wh-what?" Avery sniffled, struggling to understand.

Jaylen pointed behind him toward the lobby. "That's what Paige said in the bathroom."

"How do you know what she said?" Avery's instincts went on high alert. There was no way Jaylen had overheard their conversation from the auditorium. What kind of stunt was the ghost up to now?

Tyler sighed. "At least here you'll all be together forever."

"Forever young," Jaylen said.

"Forever playing games."

"Forever best friends."

"Poor Maddie has been sooooo lonely." Jaylen pretended to wipe a tear from his cheek.

Avery gawked at them. Why were they talking like that? "You're not Maddie?" Her voice quivered. "Who are you?"

"Ah, she figured it out. Smart girl," Jaylen said. He clapped his hands.

"What's the point of growing up, anyway?" Tyler's eyebrows raised so high, they vanished under his shaggy bangs. "You certainly weren't looking forward to it."

"What?" Avery whispered.

"Yes, giving up is actually the right thing to do. Because nothing really matters," Jaylen said cheerfully.

"So, why try?" Tyler added.

Avery recoiled. That was a terrible thing to say. She'd

never thought that way, had she? She would never be that negative, right?

Right?

"Life is meaningless," Jaylen said.

"Whoever we are, we all end up the same," Tyler said, nodding.

"Buried in the ground."

"Dead and gone."

Something about the way they were talking sounded familiar to Avery.

She gasped. Her mom had said the skull's purpose in the story was to make Hamlet realize that no matter your position in life, prince or clown, everyone ended up the same. Dead and buried.

Tyler and Jayden had started freaking out after touching the skull. Avery and her friends weren't only trapped in the Old Winter Playhouse with a ghost. There was another force. An evil force.

The skull itself.

The skull was toying with them, tempting them to touch it so that through the physical connection it could invade their minds. Avery thought back to Jaylen's fascination with it on the stage. Later she'd heard the piano music in the auditorium that had drawn her into the hall to investigate. If Paige and Tyler hadn't returned when they did, Avery might have gone onstage and picked up the skull, too. Since that hadn't worked, the skull had come to them, surprising them in the dressing room, prompting Tyler to grab it and stow it away.

Then it had gone to the lobby, and Paige had almost been its next victim.

"Why are you torturing us?" Avery whispered.

Jaylen's face hardened. "I hate children."

"Why shouldn't your life get cut short, like mine was?" Tyler jeered.

"No use leaving here, Avery," Jaylen said. "You didn't even try to like your new home. You gave up—Paige said so."

"You're good at that, right?" Tyler taunted. "Give up now."

"Life is pointless, anyway," Jaylen said.

A wave of nausea swamped Avery. No. That was wrong. When they'd watched the *Hamlet* movie, her mom had made it clear that the skull symbolized how money and status didn't mean anything in the end, that people were equal, no matter if they were rich or poor. This skull had warped that belief into something horrific.

It believed that life itself didn't matter.

Now that everything was about to be taken from her, Avery realized how lucky she was. She had so much to live for, and so did her friends. Travel, new experiences, adventures, the list went on.

Tyler grinned a nasty smile. "Ashes to ashes . . ."

"Dust to dust," Jaylen finished.

The wind rattled in the vent above the stage. An idea sparked in Avery's brain. Trying to break the skull hadn't worked. But maybe there was another way to get rid of it.

She checked her phone. She should have enough time.

It would be risky. She might not succeed.

Still, she had to try to save her friends. And herself. They each had a whole life to live. She'd have to step out of her comfort zone, face her own fears, and be a leader for the first time ever.

But Avery had faced and overcome horrible challenges in the last few hours. She was the one who had led her friends to find the key. She'd realized what was happening onstage and tried to stop Jaylen from falling into the grave. She was the one who'd figured out the skull's evil intentions. Maybe she was braver and stronger than she believed.

Maybe Paige was right. She hadn't really tried to make things work in Philly. Maybe if she *really* tried, she could do anything.

Avery wiped away her tears. A sense of calm settled over her. She stood and gathered her backpack from where she'd ditched it earlier. "I'm going to see if I can find anything to eat."

Tyler and Jaylen glanced at each other and shrugged. "Sure. Good luck with that," Tyler said.

Avery strode up the aisle toward the lobby. She had a plan to destroy the skull and get them out of the Old Winter Playhouse at the same time.

CHAPTER SIXTEEN

BURSTING INTO THE LOBBY, AVERY NOTICED THE SKULL OUT of the corner of her eye, still present in the wreckage of the display case. She kept her attention straight ahead and strode purposefully toward the office. It might be silly, but she didn't want to risk making "eye" contact with the skull. What if it could see into her soul or something? She couldn't risk it somehow discovering her scheme. Ignoring it had to be best.

Inside the office, Avery beelined to the Lost and Found box and knelt on the floor.

"Please, please, please . . . ," she whispered.

She snagged the red purse, dug out the pack of cigarettes, and flipped it over. A tiny detail from the old days spying on the Redmonds had stuck with her. There, slipped between the cellophane wrapping and the carton, was a matchbook. Yes! But she couldn't let herself celebrate yet. She removed the matchbook from the wrapper and opened the cover. Some of the matches were gone. Four remained.

Relief washed over her. Now for item number two. Avery rose to her feet and studied the nearest desk. There had to be something she could use. She grabbed a small bottle of hand sanitizer lying on its side next to a discarded candy wrapper. Then she gathered a stack of paper from the nearby printer and slid it into the main compartment of her backpack. That was item number three. She left the zipper open for item number four.

Returning to the lobby, Avery warily approached the display case, a nervous sweat breaking out over her body. She set her backpack on the floor and pushed the main compartment open as wide as possible. Grabbing the fallen broom by its bristles, she took aim. No way was she going to touch the skull and let it invade her mind.

In one swift motion, Avery skewered it through the right eye socket, wincing, waiting for a cry of outrage. The skull remained silent. Avery pitched it into her open backpack. It gaped at her as she zipped the compartment and shut it inside.

Time to implement her strategy. Avery pushed back her shoulders and straightened her posture, hoping to project confidence. She entered the auditorium.

Both boys swiveled their heads around to face her.

"Whatcha up to, Aves?" Jaylen asked.

"You know anything you try won't work," Tyler said.

Ignoring them both, Avery marched down the aisle. As she passed Paige, her heart skipped a beat. Her friend was conscious.

Paige reached out and clasped Avery's hand. "What are you doing?" Her skin was cold, her lips white and cracked.

Avery leaned close. "I'm getting us rescued."

Paige's forehead crinkled with worry. "How?" she whispered.

Avery hesitated. Paige would try to talk her out of it if she knew the plan. Avery squeezed her fingers. "Don't stress. It'll be fine."

"Please be careful," Paige said.

"I will," Avery said, brimming with emotion. "I'm so sorry, I never meant to—"

"It's okay. I'm sorry, too." Paige's eyes glistened. All her mascara had worn off, and she looked like the little girl Avery had met in day care. "Let's just get through this."

"Girls!"

Both Avery and Paige froze. The boys had uttered the word simultaneously, Tyler's deep bass under Jaylen's higher voice.

"What are you two cooking up?" Again, the two spoke in unison, as if the skull had given up pretending Jaylen and Tyler were still their own individuals and decided to talk through both of them at the same time.

A chill slithered up Avery's spine. She faked a re-assuring smile at Paige, raised her chin, and continued toward the stage without answering.

"Come sit with us, Avery," the voices continued. The two tones clashed and grated together like discordant harmony in a song, hurting her ears.

These are not my friends talking, she reminded herself as she climbed the steps to the stage. *This is the skull try-ing to trick me.*

"Where you going?" the boys called.

Avery crossed in front of the tombstone and passed the ghost light. As she followed the damaged cord to the far wings, she hoped with every bit of strength she had it would hold together. If the ghost light failed and she had to confront both Maddie's ghost and the evil skull, she didn't know how she'd ever save her friends.

Beyond the side curtains in the wings, a ladder made of metal piping clung to the brick wall and ascended into the gloom above. Avery took a deep breath, turned off her cell light, and shoved the phone into her back pocket. She waited a moment for her eyes to adjust to the dimness. Barely enough light filtered in from the stage, but it would have to do. She started to climb.

"Better see what she's up to," the boys said.

Avery's foot slipped on a rung, and she clutched the sides of the ladder, gasping in terror. She slowed her pace. At one point she had to pause and swipe her sweaty palms on her T-shirt to make sure they didn't slide off the metal, making her plummet to the stage below. She imagined herself falling, floating free and easy for a split second before striking the hard floor like Maddie had—

She cut off the thought. *Stop it.*

Avery finally made it to the top of the ladder and onto the catwalk. On the stage below, Tyler crossed his arms and sneered at her.

"Well, well, well. Aren't we brave." The boys' voices remained synched, though Jaylen, stuck in the audience, sounded fainter.

Eyes ahead, stay focused. Avery made her way to the middle of the catwalk. In the ceiling, at least twelve feet higher still, the gray lines of light around the vent were growing brighter. Dawn was near.

"Avery?" Paige's voice sounded weak.

"It's okay," Avery called. "I'm fine."

"This ought to be entertaining," the boys mocked.

The wind rattled in the vent. A cool breeze touched Avery's cheek, and she lifted her face to gulp in the fresh air. With new determination, she knelt and carefully dumped the skull from the backpack to the iron floor of the catwalk. It landed with a muted clunk.

The boys cackled. "Good luck with whatever you're doing."

Avery gritted her teeth. She crumpled up several sheets of paper, then squirted hand sanitizer on the resulting wads. Convinced all would be lost if her skin even brushed the bone, she gingerly placed the paper on the edge of the skull's left eye socket and used the useless butane lighter from the séance to shove it farther inside. She clicked the switch on the lighter several times, just in case, but it didn't work.

"Do you really think you can beat me?" the boys called. "How adorable."

Avery finished stuffing the skull with paper. She opened the matchbook with quivering fingers, picturing a flame nipping at her skin, scorching her hand, blazing up her arms. What if she got burned again? What if her gamble didn't succeed? What if she was wrong about the skull?

"No," Avery hissed. She had to at least try to complete her mission and save them all. She had no other choice.

She tore out a match and struck it against the rough strip at the bottom of the matchbook. It didn't spark. She tried again. No luck. She made a third attempt, the acrid smell of burnt sulfur invading her nose. It failed.

"Oh, I get it now," the boys said. "You can do it!"

Avery wondered how long Paige could hold on. She pictured a pool of blood forming under her seat in the auditorium, streaming along the floor until it splashed against the orchestra pit wall. She fought the image and tried another match. It didn't light, either. She struck it again and again, until the red tip turned black and there was no doubt it was useless.

"This isn't going to work!" The boys giggled.

Avery's hands trembled so violently she almost

dropped the matchbook. She ripped out the second to last match and struck it. It sparked. The scar on her elbow throbbed with pain. She hurled the match at the skull.

A feeble flame flared, curling around an edge of paper.

The skull lurched and rolled toward the side of the catwalk. Avery instinctively reached out, catching it right before it toppled over the edge to the stage below.

She sucked in a breath. "Oh no." She dropped the skull, but it was too late.

A cackle echoed inside her head. *Ooooh, now I'm in!* said the same high-pitched whisper Avery recognized from the phone in the ticket booth. Her hands flew to her ears in a hopeless attempt to block the voice from her mind.

Hmmmm, it seems you have a bad history with fire! How convenient! You've already set this up for me. I can't thank you enough.

"Stop it!" Avery yelled.

The flame stagnated and died inside the skull.

There is one more match! the voice snarled. *Try again, Avery! I want to watch you face your fear. It will be a disaster, I'm sure.*

"Why are you doing this?" Avery cried.

Maddie was afraid of heights. But she couldn't stand my

taunts and just haaaaad to prove how brave she was. You should've seen her fight me. Oh wait. You did see it.

Avery felt sick. So that's why Maddie had climbed to the catwalk all those years ago. During the séance, the ghost *had* been reenacting its death. She thought back to the horrifying vision of the girl pacing desperately back and forth. The agonizing sound of her yelling that she wasn't afraid of heights. How she'd pushed herself up onto the railing.

It was so easy to frighten her into losing her balance.

Avery couldn't blink away the tears pooling in her eyes.

Below her, the boys hooted, their glee impossible to deny.

The ghost light flickered and abruptly went out, plunging the building into darkness. Tyler and Jaylen roared with laughter. Paige whimpered. Inside the skull, the flame faded away.

Avery panicked. But she'd come this far. She couldn't abandon her plan. Her friends needed her. In the pitch dark, she fumbled for the last match.

You'll burn! You'll burn!

Maddie's ghost materialized on the other end of the catwalk, its face contorted with rage.

Oh look, the skull's voice taunted. *We're not alone.*

Avery despaired. What would the ghost do to her now? They'd already enraged it with the séance. The worst-case scenario had come to pass—she had to deal with both the ghost and the skull. How could she face two evils at the same time?

You can't do it, can you?

Avery gathered every ounce of mental strength she had, trying to ignore everything but the task in front of her. She struck the last match. A tiny flame erupted.

You'll burn!

Avery shoved the match at the skull. The paper in its eye socket flickered and caught fire. She held her breath as a thin trail of smoke slid up toward the vent. Yes!

The flame stagnated.

She blew on it, practically hyperventilating, yet still it fizzled until it was only a pinprick of a spark.

"No, no, no!" she whispered.

She had failed.

Suddenly, the ghost charged at her. Avery scuttled backward as it whooshed over the skull—then doubled back, whirling itself into a tornado, its gale force reigniting the flame. The fire roared greedily, devouring the oxygen. The skull shrieked, filling Avery's head and the entire theater with a piercing cry of anguish.

Maddie's ghost soared up to the vent, taking the smoke with her. Its eyes met Avery's.

"Get out!" it wailed.

In that moment, Avery understood.

Maddie's ghost had never been furious about the séance or the kids disturbing its rest.

It had been trying to protect them from the skull's evil.

The ghost rushed toward Avery again, the force of its wind pushing the skull over the edge of the catwalk. The ghastly shriek escalated into a howl as the skull plunged downward, tongues of flame licking from between its teeth and jutting from its eye sockets until it crashed on the electric cord below. The drop cloth ignited.

Avery grabbed her backpack and skidded down the ladder as fast as she could. Tyler cowered at the brink of the wings, fire building onstage behind him.

"What's happening?" His voice was his own again, but his expression was dazed, as if he was coming out of a trance.

"Run!" yelled Avery.

Tyler pivoted just as Maddie's ghost descended to hover above the building inferno, her wind fanning the flames and forcing smoke to pour toward the vent.

"No!" He backed into the wings.

"Get out!" roared Maddie's ghost.

"She's helping us, Tyler!" Avery grabbed his hand. "Let's go!"

The ghost blasted up to the roof, billows of smoke streaming with it. Understanding dawned on Tyler's face, and he let Avery drag him forward. As they ran past the fiery lump that was the skull, it exploded with a bang.

Burn! hissed the voice in her head. The fire blazed, and a flame surged at her, almost searing her bare arm. She faltered and cried out, breaking contact with Tyler. She was going to get burned again. Her backpack slipped from her shoulders onto the floor, but she didn't care. Acrid smoke filled her nose. "I can't!"

"I got you!" Tyler pulled her away from the fire and down the stairs.

On the second to last step, a *crack* came from above. Avery's gaze shot up. A grimacing gargoyle head plummeted straight at them. She shoved Tyler forward and lurched after him to the auditorium floor. The gargoyle narrowly missed her and slammed into the stairs behind her, smashing into pieces.

Jaylen, confused, struggled to rise from his seat. Tyler sped to his side. "Dude, we gotta get out of here!"

Avery raced to Paige, who was already standing on her one good leg. "Can you walk?"

"I'll try!"

Smoke swirled in their path as the four of them limped and scrabbled up the aisle, coughing and choking. Heat built behind them. From the walls, the eyes of the painted horses glowed red and menacing. At the door to the lobby, Avery peered back at the stage.

The tombstones blazed and the floorboards burned. The ghost light's bulb glowed orange and shattered, bursting into a million pieces. Maddie's ghost hung above the fire watching them, this time her mouth forming unmistakably into a smile.

"Go! Live!" she called in a triumphant voice before she lifted out of sight.

Avery, Paige, Tyler, and Jaylen bolted into the lobby to the wail of sirens and the welcome thwack of a firefighter's ax striking the boards covering the front door.

EPILOGUE
TWO WEEKS LATER

LAILA PULLED HER RUSTY SEDAN INTO THE OLD WINTER
Playhouse driveway and switched off the ignition.

"Y'all go do whatever you're doing," she said. "You
have ten minutes before we need to leave for the airport."
She slid lower in the driver's seat and lost herself in text
messages.

Avery and Tyler exited the car first. As they waited patiently in the August afternoon sun for Paige and Jaylen,
Avery eyed the building in front of them. An orange construction fence surrounded it, plastered with paper per-
mits and signs reading No Trespassing and Condemned.
Its brick exterior was intact, and the front doors and

the lobby's high windows were covered with brand-new boards. But Avery knew the walls inside had water and smoke damage, and the stage was blackened and collapsed into the basement.

Paige gingerly climbed out of the car, the stitches on her leg stiff even after two weeks. Jaylen took a moment longer, the awkward ankle boot on his lower left leg hindering his movements. Before standing, he leaned back toward the front seat console.

"Can't forget these," he said, grabbing a late-summer bouquet of black-eyed Susans and zinnias.

Laila gave him the side eye. "You better have gotten permission from Mom to pick those from her garden."

"Are you kidding?" Jaylen bobbed his head, making his braids bounce. "I can't even breathe now without asking her first."

Avery smiled ruefully. This trip to the airport was the first time any of them had been allowed to leave Ridge Road since they'd been rescued. They were all in a heap of trouble for lying to their families, sneaking out at night, and entering an abandoned building. The only reason her parents hadn't immediately whisked her back to Philadelphia was because they had a prepaid trip to take Julia to Disney World. But a punishment of some kind awaited Avery when she got home. And she deserved it.

As the four friends tromped through the weeds toward the road, a swell of gratitude overwhelmed Avery. They had all survived their night of terror.

Brandon Sernett's cross-country coach had called 911 when he and the team had spotted smoke pouring from the roof vent of the theater on their morning run. Avery had gambled on the fact that the team would run their early morning practice on the paths of Crawley Woods. And thank goodness she'd won that bet.

Each of them had come out of the theater dehydrated and shaken but otherwise healthy, except for the injuries. Luckily, Paige had lost only one pint of blood. Jaylen's ankle was severely sprained but not broken. He and Tyler suffered no ill effects from the skull's possession of them—in fact, they couldn't remember anything about it.

Avery had tried to explain to the authorities that she'd started the fire to alert the world to their desperate situation and destroy the skull at the same time. But no evidence of the matches, paper, hand sanitizer, cigarette pack, or red purse could be found. In fact, the candles, the butane lighter, and even the backpacks had mysteriously vanished without a trace. The skull itself had disappeared, not the tiniest bone fragment or heap of ash left behind. The fire department's preliminary investigation determined that the damaged extension cord, likely chewed by a rat, had caused the fire.

There was no explanation for any of this. But Avery liked to think Maddie's ghost was the culprit, still taking care of them.

Avery, Paige, Jaylen, and Tyler stopped when they reached Maddie's memorial. In the weeks since the little display had shown up, sun and rain had faded the ink on the We Remember poster. The teddy bear was facedown in the dirt. The half-dozen flower arrangements had wilted. Most of the silver helium balloons tied to a stake in the ground had shriveled, though one valiantly floated in the air, barely inflated.

Jaylen carefully propped his bouquet against the stake. "For you, Maddie," he said solemnly.

"*We* know you were there," added Tyler. "Even if no one believes us."

Though neither of them recalled the evil spirit

possessing them, both of the boys vividly remembered Maddie's ghost, the demented skull, and coming to their senses in the burning theater.

Absolutely no one—not their parents, not the authorities, not even their siblings—believed the kids' claims about the ghost and the skull. At first, Brandon had listened, but soon even he decided their account was too far-fetched to be true. Instead, everyone chalked up their story to the trauma of getting trapped in an abandoned theater rumored to be haunted.

"I think that ghosts and pure evil like the skull are just too disturbing for most people to accept," said Avery, straightening the teddy bear. "No one wants to think about mystical dark forces in the world."

"I wish I knew why the skull was so mean," Paige said. A soft breeze lifted her long curly hair around her head.

"I've been thinking about that," Avery said. "You know the play program I found in the dressing room? And the weird props master I told you about?"

"Yeah, the one who liked to collect authentic stuff to use as props," Jaylen said. "We already know that the skull was real."

"Okay, remember the trunk that was in the prop room?"

Tyler tipped his head to one side. "The one you said had, like, Boston stuff in it?"

"Right. It had a Red Sox pennant." Avery straightened her glasses on her nose. "But it also had other stuff that could be from Massachusetts, like Puritan hats and this little black pot, which I now think was the cauldron the props master talked about in the program."

They all frowned at her, perplexed.

Avery forged on. "Jaylen and Tyler, when you guys were possessed and the skull was talking through you, it said how much it hated kids."

Tyler ran his fingers through his unruly hair. "What does any of that have to do with Massachusetts?"

"Well, I did some research online this morning before Paige woke up. About Salem, Massachusetts, you know, where they had the witch trials hundreds of years ago. Guess who started all the trouble by accusing their neighbors of being witches?" Avery waited expectantly for an answer.

"I read about that once," Paige said. "Wasn't it young girls or teenagers?"

"Exactly!" Avery clapped her hands together. "So, what if the skull actually belonged to one of the people hung as a witch?"

"Bruh, what?" Jaylen said. He squinted at her like she was talking gibberish.

"Think about it. The skull just targeted kids. Maybe it was getting its revenge!"

Paige raised her eyebrows. "I guess whether you were a witch or not, getting thrown in jail like that would be enough to make you hate kids," she said. "And then if you'd been put to death, you'd definitely want revenge."

"Hmmmm," Tyler said. "Do you think the props master knew where the skull was from?"

"No clue," Avery said.

"Does it really matter?" Paige asked. "What happened to us happened."

"True," Avery agreed. As usual, Paige had a point.

"Okay, this is making my brain hurt," Jaylen said. "I'm just glad it's all over."

The owners of the theater and the parents came to a mutual agreement not to sue each other. There was enough blame to go around on both sides. Of course, the kids shouldn't have gone into the theater. But the owners hadn't properly secured or maintained the building, making it an accident waiting to happen. Or an "attractive nuisance," according to lawyers.

Everyone just wanted to move on.

"My mom says the theater is being torn down next month," Tyler said. "The owners finally settled with Maddie's parents."

They all regarded the memorial.

"It's so sad she died so young," Paige said.

Jaylen sighed. "And she was so brave, helping us out."

"What do you think will happen to her ghost?" asked Paige. She twirled the friendship bracelet around her wrist, the one Avery made for her. The bracelet from Bethany Barnes was on her other wrist. They hadn't gone to Bethany's for a sleepover, but they had talked to her one night in the Sernetts' front yard. Bethany had apologized to Avery for her past bullying. And Avery had accepted her apology. She realized now that people could change for the better.

"I think Maddie's ghost just stayed around to protect other kids from the skull attacking them, like it had attacked her," Avery said. "Now that the skull is gone and they're tearing down the building, I think she'll be at peace."

"I hope so." Tyler said.

"Maybe we should say something," suggested Paige.

"Like what?" asked Jaylen.

"Like thank you."

"Well, I want to thank Avery," Jaylen said, playfully patting the top of her head. "I mean, you were the one smart enough to save us all."

"I can't imagine how afraid you must've been," said Paige.

"I absolutely was," Avery admitted. She contemplated her best friends with a mix of emotion. Affection for them. Sadness she was leaving. Dread for whatever punishment was coming for her back in Philadelphia.

Mostly she felt happy for the surprising strength she'd discovered within herself that terrifying night they'd been trapped in the theater. She'd saved them all. She hadn't let her fears drag her down.

"Okay, how about we just have a moment of silence," Tyler said.

"Yes, perfect," said Paige.

Avery closed her eyes. *Thank you, Maddie. Your kindness won't be for nothing. I'll do my best to live a good life and appreciate everything I have.*

A blaring honk ruined the moment. Laila was laying on the horn.

"Ah, man, we'd better get going," Jaylen laughed.

He and Tyler took off for the car, and the girls trailed behind.

"I'm so glad they're getting along better," Avery said.

"Right?" Paige agreed.

She and Jaylen had decided to just be friends. He was already interested in a girl he met at sports camp in June, another basketball player. Avery wasn't sure what would happen with Tyler, but no way would she betray his confidence and let Paige know he liked her.

Paige, for her part, didn't know who she liked.

"It's confusing," she'd told Avery during one late-night talk. Her new, self-assured attitude that confounded Avery so much had slipped at that moment, giving a glimpse of the vulnerability underneath. "Maybe I'm just not ready to be interested in anyone."

"That's okay," Avery had said. "We're only thirteen. We have a lot of time left."

And they did.

She and Paige had pledged to be more open with each other, so any bad feelings wouldn't fester. Avery would be a better listener, and Paige would let her know when she needed to talk.

Avery had made another decision. She planned to

tell her mom about how her worries often got out of control and almost paralyzed her. She'd faced her worst fears in the theater, from fire to a ghost to evil itself, and made it through. Her belief in herself had grown, which was fantastic. But too many times that awful night, her imagination had created even more horrors to worry about, stuff that never ended up happening at all. She wanted to stop doing that. She probably needed to talk to a therapist.

"I have an idea," Paige said as they neared Laila's car. "Have you heard of Agatha Christie?"

"Yeah," Avery said. "She's a famous writer, right?"

"Yup, she wrote, like, a hundred murder mysteries back in the day. Natalie loves her. Says the plots are really twisty. How about, instead of the new Lark and Ivy, we read an Agatha Christie mystery together and try to solve the murder before her detective in the story does?"

Avery considered this. It had gotten way too easy for her to guess the end of the Lark and Ivy books anyway. It was time for a change. She smiled. "That sounds great."

As she climbed into the car, Avery's phone buzzed. She checked the screen. There was a text from a number she didn't recognize.

Hey Avery it's Maya. Your mom gave me your number. You want see that movie the séance with me when you get back? Let me know!

Avery stifled a giggle. She would never see that movie, she was sure. But she'd find another movie to go to with Maya, she decided.

And she couldn't wait.

ACKNOWLEDGMENTS

This book came together quickly, and a lot of people helped that happen. Thanks so much to the talented team at Delacorte Press/Random House Children's Books: Tamar Schwartz, managing editor; Colleen Fellingham, copy editor; Amanda Hong, copy editor; CJ Han, production manager; Jade Rector, cover and interior designer; Emma Swan, proofreader; Lena Reilly, publicist; and especially Alison Romig, editor. Ali, I'm so grateful for your faith in my writing ability. Working with you is so easy and an absolute joy.

I adore the cover illustration by artist Matt Schu. Thank you, Matt, for bringing the abandoned stage at the Old Winter Playhouse to spooky life.

To Karyn Fischer, my wonderful former agent, who helped jump-start my writing career, thank you. And to

Hilary Harwell, my new agent, I'm beyond excited to work with you.

Three debut author groups have been a wellspring of resources, information, and support for me since fall 2022: 2023 Debut Authors, MG in 23, and Class of 2k23 Books. I don't know how I could've navigated my debut year and beyond without them. In particular, authors Gigi Griffiths, Alena Bruzas, Kara H. L. Chen, and Federico Erebia, I appreciate your friendship and support beyond measure.

Several brilliant, established authors were kind enough to blurb my debut and I didn't get to thank them in my past acknowledgments, so I will now. Kiersten White, Dan Poblocki, Lindsay Currie, and Lorien Lawrence, thank you so much for reading and boosting a debut author. Your kindness truly means the world to me! And to writer Sarah Van Goethem, I appreciate so much that you dropped everything and read an early draft of this book in one day! Thank you for giving your time and insights.

I'm fortunate to have amazing friends in my life. The encouragement I've gotten from them in the last few years (whether I know them from neighborhoods past or present, or from college, high school, grade school, or even preschool!) has been overwhelming. Thank you, thank you, thank you for cheering me on.

My family near and far are fantastic. I particularly value my husband, Ted, who patiently listened to me read not one but two versions of this book out loud. I couldn't have written this book without his support.

And to the booksellers, librarians, teachers, and reviewers who have championed my books—I'm grateful to each and every one of you.

ONE

Rebecca fought to keep her eyes open as she peered across the living room into the dim kitchen. The glowing numbers on the microwave clock read 12:00. Midnight. She sighed and sank deeper into the couch. The way she figured it, the later she stayed awake, the slower time would move—and the longer it would feel until she had to leave home. She dug a handful of hot popcorn from the bowl in her lap and crammed it into her mouth.

On the TV screen a young girl crept through a dark graveyard full of crumbling tombstones. A ghostly figure followed her, reaching out a bony hand. Creepy organ music surged.

"*Run!*" Rebecca whispered.

Two sharp taps exploded in the quiet behind her. Rebecca jerked in surprise, making popcorn fly from the bowl. She hit the mute button on the remote, her heart pounding. Silence. Her eyes swept the small, cluttered room and the entryway piled with suitcases. Nothing moved. No sound came from Mom's room above.

Okay. Her ears must be playing tricks on her. She turned back to the TV.

The tapping came again, this time in a staccato rhythm Rebecca had heard a kazillion times. She dropped the remote, leapt to her feet, and raced to the front door. Through the peephole she spied a shadowy figure hovering on the stoop, a silhouette of braids cascading from under a ball cap. She cracked open the door.

"You scared the heck outta me," she hissed.

"Ha!" Rebecca's best friend, Jenna, grabbed her arm and pulled her outside into the sticky summer night. "Gotcha."

"Shhhh!" Rebecca closed the door behind her. "My mom doesn't know I'm up."

"Please. She'd sleep through a tornado." Jenna pushed a silver gift bag into Rebecca's hands. "I totally forgot to give this to you before."

A warm glow spread through Rebecca's chest. "What is it?"

"Something for your car trip tomorrow. In case you

get bored with your mom and her eighties music." Even in the faint light, Jenna's brown eyes sparkled with mischief.

Rebecca's warm glow sputtered and died. "Don't remind me."

She was leaving the next day to spend the rest of the summer babysitting her two-year-old cousin at an Iowa farmhouse. Meanwhile, Jenna would be riding horses, water-skiing, and basically having a blast at Camp Birchdale. It wasn't fair.

"Come on, it won't be that bad," Jenna said. "Your aunt and uncle sound cool."

"How would I know?" Rebecca muttered. "It's not like they've bothered with me in forever."

Jenna planted her hands on her hips. "You promised you'd give them a chance."

"Yeah, yeah." Rebecca picked at her thumbnail. Hanging out with Uncle Jon, Aunt Sylvie, and their little boy, Justin, was nice in theory, but in reality it was too little, too late. This reunion, or whatever it was, should have happened when she was young and begging to see Dad's side of the family. Now she was older and had things to do. Like go to Cubs games in the city or ride her bike to the beach.

Or go to camp with her best friend.

"You don't fool me." Jenna gave her a no-nonsense look. "I know you're curious about them. Now open your present."

"Yes, ma'am." Rebecca dug into the bag and pulled out a heavy paperback book. On the cover was a black-and-white sketch of a dead tree looming over a misty cornfield. She tipped the book toward the streetlight and read the title: *Heart-Stopping Heartland Hauntings.* The letters shimmered and dripped with red bloodlike splatters. A delicious shiver crawled up her spine. "Awesome."

"Look on the bright side," Jenna said. "You've always wanted to see a ghost. An old farmhouse in the middle of nowhere is the perfect place."

"I guess." Rebecca mulled this over. She hadn't really thought of it that way. Jenna was always so much more positive than she was.

The rumble of a loose tailpipe erupted, and a black car cruised along the street. Both girls shrank back, plastering themselves into the shadows. The car turned at the end of the block and headed to the alley behind the houses. Jenna's brother was home from his job delivering pizzas.

"Go, before you get in trouble." Rebecca threw her arms around Jenna. "I'm going to miss you so much."

"I wish you were coming with me." Jenna's voice was

muffled against Rebecca's shoulder. "I can't believe the next time we see each other, we'll be in junior high."

Rebecca's throat tightened, cutting off the *goodbye* she wanted to say. Jenna pulled away and hopped down the stairs, braids flying. Rebecca watched through tears as her friend disappeared into the small brick bungalow next door. The upcoming six weeks were going to be the worst. She and Jenna hadn't been apart for more than eight days since kindergarten.

"What are you doing?"

Rebecca whirled around. Mom stood in the doorway wrapped in a white bathrobe, her blond hair in a messy ponytail, eyes sleepy behind crooked glasses.

"Nothing," Rebecca said. "Jenna dropped off a present for me."

She pulled the book to her chest, but it was too late. Mom had already scanned the title.

"Seriously? Jenna of all people should know better." Mom crossed her arms. "I thought you were over this ghost obsession. We do not need a repeat of last summer's fiasco."

Rebecca lifted her chin. "How were we supposed to know Mrs. Alvarado's son was in town? And why would he walk around an empty house with a flashlight in the middle of the night?"

"Why would you try to break into a house to prove it was haunted?" Mom shot back. She lifted a shaky hand and smoothed a flyaway wisp of hair from her eyes. "I was absolutely terrified to get a call from the police at two a.m. You girls are lucky you didn't get arrested. Or hurt."

"But it was totally spooky the way the light flickered and the footsteps—"

"There are no such things as ghosts," Mom said through clenched teeth.

How do you know? Rebecca wanted to yell. She bit her tongue instead. Lately, she and Mom had been arguing more than usual. Jenna said fighting with your parents was a normal part of growing up, but it made Rebecca queasy. She and Mom had been the perfect team the past six years, just the two of them, together. But lately it seemed they were always on opposite sides.

Rebecca ran her fingers over the raised letters on the book's cover. "This is only for fun. But I guess you don't want me to have any of that."

Mom clicked her tongue. "Honey, that's not true." She peered over the top of her glasses at Rebecca. "Have you been crying?"

"Not really." Rebecca ducked her head, letting her hair fall in a brown, curly curtain around her face.

"Oh, Co-Cap." Co-Cap was Mom's nickname for her, short for *co-captain*. She put her arm around Rebecca's shoulder and guided her into the house. "I'm sorry you're not going with Jenna this summer. We just can't afford—"

"I know." Rebecca sniffed, squirming with guilt. Mom always worried about money. "It's fine."

"I promise, when I get my raise next year, I'll send you to camp, okay?"

Rebecca nodded. When Mom got her PhD, she would make more money as a high school English teacher, money they could really use. Summer break was her time to finish her dissertation. So when Jon and Sylvie had invited them to Iowa, offering her a quiet place to focus on writing, Mom had been thrilled. Then they'd agreed to pay Rebecca to watch little Justin while they worked and got ready for their new baby. All that, plus the chance to get to know each other better and—*bam!*—the decision had been made. Mom called it a "win-win." Rebecca wasn't so sure.

"We'll make this summer as fun as possible for you," Mom continued. "We'll go to county fairs and take bike rides and your uncle Jon scouted out a local pool not far away. It won't be all babysitting, okay?"

"I guess." Rebecca forced a weak smile.

"All right, turn off the TV and go to bed please." Mom

planted a kiss on Rebecca's cheek. "We need to wake up early."

"Okay." Rebecca didn't fight her. She'd watched the scary movie before and knew how it ended. Plus, she had *Heart-Stopping Heartland Hauntings* to keep her awake and her mind off the next day.

Upstairs in her room, Rebecca flipped a switch, turning on the dozens of twinkling lights strung across the ceiling. She swept a mass of colorful pillows from the bed, climbed between the sheets, and opened her new book. The table of contents listed fantastically eerie titles like "Beware the Banshee of Beloit" and "What Lurks in Devil's Backbone Park?" She snuggled in and flipped to chapter one, "The Phantom of Full Moon Lake." The first sentence stopped her cold.

Young, open-minded believers are the people most likely to encounter a ghost.

She bit her lip. That described her to the core. So why hadn't she seen one yet?

"Lights off, please," Mom called from across the hall.

Rebecca snapped shut the book and tossed it on the pillow next to her. Fine. She'd read on the car trip. Reaching to turn off the lights, her hand bumped the small oval picture frame that sat on her nightstand. She picked it up. The picture inside showed Dad holding her when she was six years old, a week before he'd passed away. Their cheeks were pressed together, their eyes the exact same round shape and hazel color with thick lashes. Rebecca had given up ever meeting his ghost—he would have shown himself by now if he was ever going to. Plus, she'd done the research. Ghosts were spirits of people who had died violently or were out for revenge. Dad had passed peacefully and surrounded by family, from a heart condition he'd had his whole life. Nothing unexpected.

Rebecca set the picture on top of *Heart-Stopping Heartland Hauntings*, so she'd remember to take it to Iowa, and switched off the lights. Jenna could be right. A farmhouse over a hundred years old could be the perfect spot for a ghost. If she got lucky, this summer might actually be exciting.

Maybe she'd find her own "heart-stopping haunting."

ABOUT THE AUTHOR

WENDY PARRIS is the author of *Field of Screams*, a Junior Library Guild Gold Star Selection, and *Stage Fright*. She has always loved telling stories, so she studied film at Northwestern University, acted in small Chicago theaters after graduation, and even created tales on the spot as part of an improv comedy troupe. Now she writes spooky books for tweens and teens. She lives in Illinois with her family in an old house that is probably not haunted.

WENDYPARRIS.COM